D0021134

IN THE RIVER DARKNESS

Marlene Röder

SCARLET VOYAGE
Young Adult Fiction

Title of the German original edition(s): *Im Fluss* by Marlene Röder
© 2007 by Ravensburger Buchverlag Otto Maier GmbH, Ravensburg (Germany)
Translated from the German edition by Tammi Reichel

 The translation of this work was supported by a grant from the Goethe-Institut which is funded by the German Ministry of Foreign Affairs

LCCN: 2013933047

Röder, Marlene.

In the River Darkness / Marlene Röder.

Summary: Mia, the new girl in town by the river, starts dating Alex Stonebrook. She strikes a friendship with Jay, Alex's brother. The relationships between the characters become more complicated as Mia learns about the Stonebrooks. Jay's mysterious friend, Alina, is also jealous of Mia. Strange things start to happen, and they all seem to stem from the river.

ISBN 978-1-62324-010-3

Future editions:
Paperback ISBN: 978-1-62324-011-0
EPUB ISBN: 978-1-62324-013-4
Single-User PDF ISBN: 978-1-62324-014-1
Multi-User PDF ISBN: 978-1-62324-017-2

Printed in the United States of America
112013 Bang Printing, Brainerd, Minn.
10 9 8 7 6 5 4 3 2 1

Scarlet Voyage
Box 398, 40 Industrial Road
Berkeley Heights, NJ 07922
USA
www.scarletvoyage.com

Cover Illustration: Shutterstock.com

I listen to the river
as it tells me of its life.
As I move on I recognize:
it was my own story.

Michael Schlaadt

Introduction

|||||||||||||||||||||||||||||||||||||||||||||||||||||||||||||||||||||||||||||||||||||||||||||||||||||||||||||||||||||||||||||

Will this be the day I die?

The question bolts through my mind as I hear the ice breaking beneath my ice skates, an odd sound, like the high-pitched whining and complaining of a living creature. I cannot move. I don't even have time to scream.

The very next instant the whole world seems to fall away: our house, the riverbank, the pale winter sky . . . everything disappears with a loud splash.

The sudden cold hits me like a punch, presses the air out of my lungs. Wildly flailing my arms and legs, I fight my way to the surface. My clothing is soaked through within seconds, and the heavy skates drag my legs downward like lead weights. If I don't get rid of them right away, I won't be able to hold myself above water for very long.

Water in my eyes, my nose, my mouth. . . . I can't breathe. I can't think clearly. In a panic, I gasp for breath.

Finally! I don't know how, but I manage to kick a skate off one foot. Now, with half of the heavy weight on my feet already gone, it will be easier to lose the second one.

I am not going to die today!

Greedily, I suck in deep breaths of the clear winter air. Now I just need a plan that will get me out of this damned hole in the ice.

With great difficulty, I paddle my way over to the jagged edge of the ice. It grins at me mockingly, like the zigzag teeth of a jack-o'-lantern. Hold on tight, pull yourself up, I order my body. Come on, you can do it!

But my body doesn't want to obey me. I scream at my arms, which are too weak to hold my weight, to press me upward and back into life. My numb fingers slide off the slippery broken edge. I curse as I look for a place to get a grip, in vain.

"I . . . will not . . . die . . . today," I mutter to myself, gritting my teeth together tightly so they don't start chattering. I will not die today!

Again and again, I try until tiny black flecks flicker before my eyes. Again and again, I fail.

There is blood on the ice. My blood. My hands are cut, but I don't feel it.

I hold tight to the edge of the ice. Staying above water is the only thing that matters right now. Just take a little rest before I try again. . . . What's that noise? My teeth have started to chatter, I can't stop. . . . I'm so terribly cold. Apathetically, I look at my blood, red, so red in all the white surrounding it.

For a fraction of a second, an image of our oath flashes through my mind, the oath we sealed with blood, yet each of the three of us still broke it in our own way.

For the thousandth time I ask myself if we could have done something differently, or whether everything was leading up to it all along. . . . Damn it, even here, even in this situation, I can't stop thinking about it.

Maybe I've even earned it, to die here, because of what I did. Maybe I deserve to drown in the water of this river. I don't know.

Did it have to happen like this? *I ask myself, and my thoughts fly back to the day when everything began . . .*

LA PRIMAVERA
SPRING

Chapter 1

Mia

〰〰〰〰〰〰〰〰〰〰〰〰〰〰〰〰〰〰〰〰〰〰〰〰〰〰〰〰〰〰〰〰

"We'll be there soon, sweetie," my mother said in a cheerful voice, twisting herself around in the passenger's seat up front to face me. I ignored her and continued to stare out the window at the landscape rushing by outside: yellow-brown fields, an occasional small town, a cluster of houses huddled too close together. The naked trees and bushes seemed to duck down under the gray March sky. Could you smell the coming of spring outside? Here in the car, it just smelled like car.

For a moment, it seemed like the posts alongside the road were racing past us, while our car actually stood still. I wished my father wouldn't drive so fast.

I didn't want to get there.

"You'll see, you'll like the house," my mother said for at least the hundredth time. I was starting to wonder who she was trying to convince.

"It's right near a river, surrounded by nature . . . didn't you used to want to live in the country, Mia?"

This was true, although at the time I had been ten years old and wanted nothing more in the whole world than to have my own pony. I was just about to let her know that I could imagine something better now than rotting away in a miniscule town in the middle of nowhere, but I bit my tongue just in time. It wouldn't change anything, anyway.

It was hopeless.

A few months ago, I had ranted and raved, trying to get my parents to abandon their plans to move. I remembered my mother's tears, her plea: "Could you at least show some understanding for our situation?" And my father's silent, worried looks. He was unhappy because he was making me unhappy.

I remembered my desperate, subconscious, helpless rage. That the two of them could completely dismantle my life, just like that, any way they liked, made me raging mad. But now, after the thing with Nicolas, I'd given up the fight.

I was driftwood.

At least now I won't have to see him anymore, I thought. I didn't want to think or feel anymore. That was working really well.

My fingers played with the earplugs of my iPod. I wished we could just keep driving. Not from anywhere, not headed anywhere.

With each mile, I left my old life in the city farther behind—playing cello in the youth orchestra, meeting my friends and hanging out at the mall, or sneaking into parties thrown by cooler people that we weren't even invited to. Okay, it might not have been fabulous, but it was my life!

But then one day, my father was offered this amazing job as head of an advertising agency. He wanted the job. My mother agreed, under one condition: we wouldn't live in the city but in a small town outside it instead.

"A little house in the country, Mia," she said with gleaming eyes. "I've always dreamed of it."

My protests had no weight against my parents' ideas. I was young, after all, and would get used to our new life in no time.

No one asked what I dreamed of.

Driftwood.

The clouds hung low in the sky, and soon it would start to rain. My father turned into a smaller street.

"Have I already told you that two boys around your age live in the house next door?" my mother asked, attempting to break the silence again. "I met them recently when your dad and I looked at the house one more time. They seemed nice, didn't they?" She put her hand on my father's shoulder.

He nodded obediently. "Hmmm."

I swallowed the bitter lump that suddenly stuck in my throat. *They have no idea . . . they don't know anything!*

The idiotic tears burned in my eyes. Again. I bit my lower lip until I tasted blood. I would rather suffocate than cry now in front of my parents!

Dad gave me a sympathetic look in the rearview mirror. I quickly stuffed the earplugs of my iPod back in my ears and turned up the volume. Vivaldi's *Springtime* from the Four Seasons resounded so loud it almost hurt. But it drowned out the sounds of the tires, my mother's voice, everything, until nothing was left but the music.

~~~~~

That must be it, I thought, twenty minutes later as our car rolled into a gravel driveway—my new home. It stood outside the town, as if it couldn't quite decide if it should join the other houses or not. In front of the house across the street, the only other one around, an old woman was working in the garden. She looked us over suspiciously as we got out of the car.

My mother was right. It really was a pretty house: two stories high with shuttered windows and a well-tended garden all around it. The first crocuses were even poking their colorful heads up through the earth. A few hundred feet behind the house I could even see the river shimmering like dull metal in the afternoon light.

"Well?" my mother asked in an expectant voice. Her eyes were beaming.

I didn't answer. All I could muster was a weak nod.

"Please don't look so gloomy," she pleaded, pressing her lips together.

"You can't expect me to find everything wonderful here right away, okay?" I hissed back. My voice cut through the spring air like a knife, and the old woman in the garden across the street looked up at us in surprise.

"No, and no one is asking you to," my father reassured in a calm tone. "But it would be nice if you would at least try. That makes it easier, you know." Then he put one arm across my mother's shoulder and the other across mine and drew us in the direction of the house. "Let's take a quick look inside first.

11

. . . I'm famished. And then we'll see if we can't find just the right room for you. What do you think of that, Mia?"

~~~~~

I picked the nicest room. It was upstairs, large, with a big window overlooking the garden. This was what it looked like, then, the efforts of my parental units to reconcile me to my forced relocation. A bribe, so to speak. Not so bad.

The furniture and the rest of our belongings wouldn't be delivered until morning, but we had brought the essentials with us. The first thing I got out of the trunk was my cello.

"You wouldn't let anyone else touch it, would you?" my father called after me, as I pressed the instrument to my chest like a shield . . . or a lover.

In my new room, I unpacked the cello and leaned it again a wall, then sat on the wooden floor in front of it. Its red body looked so beautiful in the empty room. The walls were entirely white. There was something comforting and pure about them. Everything was yet to be determined—no photos of a previous life, no memories.

Maybe it actually was possible to start over again . . .

The branches of a tree cast filigree shadows on the walls. I observed how the shadows slowly moved and changed the walls and decided not to hang anything on them.

I had no idea what I should do next. Finally, I stood up and opened the window. A large tree stood directly in front of the house and stretched its budding branches toward me, as if it wanted to welcome me with a handshake. "Hello," I said to the tree. When I leaned out the window as far as I could, I could just touch the tips of the tree.

As I did that, I noticed that I had a perfect view of the house next door from here. I studied it critically. It stood closer to the river than ours and was built of wood. It looked a little run down, somehow. I searched my pockets for a cigarette while I continued to look the house over. Not that I saw anything interesting over there, but the house had some kind of fascination for me, for whatever inexplicable reason.

The old woman with her housecoat was still standing in her front yard. Her back was as straight as the handle of the rake she held in her hand. She just stood there and stared over at the bank of the little river. Even when it suddenly began to rain, hard, she stayed rooted to the spot and didn't move.

"Now that's strange," I thought. She was probably a little senile. I wanted to turn away from the window, bored, but there was something about her stance. Something like . . . watchfulness.

The woman peered into the bushes and vines at the edge of the river as if there were a dangerous animal crouched there that might pounce at any moment. I craned my neck— but there wasn't anything there, was there? Nothing and no one, except that slim figure in the streaming rain.

I asked myself what on earth she saw. What was she thinking about?

Rain rolled down my neck. I was so busy looking, I almost fell out the window! Out of fear, I made some noise, because the old woman suddenly turned her face in my direction. In spite of the distance between us, I couldn't help but notice her light blue eyes, like forget-me-nots. Could

13

she see me through the branches? Hesitantly, I raised my hand to wave to her.

In that moment, someone wearing a hooded shirt and carrying an umbrella came around the corner of the house. Must be her grandson, one of the "nice boys." Shaking his head, he talked with the old woman. Then he took her by the arm to guide her, while his other hand held the colorful umbrella above her. The two of them disappeared into the house.

I put out my cigarette and closed the window.

~ ~ ~ ~ ~

The first night in our new house, I lay awake for a long time, listening to my breathing, which got lost in the darkness. It seemed so foreign to me. I stretched out a hand and touched my cello, still standing against the wall next to me. Carefully, I plucked a string. The A tone vibrated for a long time in the otherwise empty room.

Only when the note faded away with a sigh did I finally fall into a dreamless sleep.

~ ~ ~ ~ ~

One well-aimed kick and the Coke can skittered over the edge of the riverbank with a satisfying clatter and splashed into the water.

I hated that river, babbling as it wended its way through town. I hated the fields with their first smatterings of green. This whole backwater idyll made me sick! It was so damn quiet here. Apart from a few squealing children playing soccer somewhere in the distance, the only thing you could hear were the birds, singing their hearts out.

Where were the cars? Where were the people? Even if there was nothing more than a bakery, a tiny outpost of a grocery store, and—wow, the high point of entertainment and culture—a small outdoor swimming pool (where nothing was swimming at the moment but last year's leaves), there still had to be at least a few people around here! But the houses stood silent in the sun as if the whole village had died out. Or had everyone left? It wouldn't have surprised me.

But anything was better than schlepping moving cartons as heavy as pianos and having to listen to my parents' upbeat commentary. My arms felt like they were as long as a gorilla's by now, and I was in dire need of a cigarette break anyway. That was reason enough to steal away and explore this hick town.

On the other hand, I hadn't seen much yet that would have been worth exploring. Even the dogs here seemed to be bored—a particularly ugly specimen trotted along behind me for a few minutes. I threw it a few of my chocolate-covered raisins, which it ate with a teeth-smacking grin. The motley stray seemed to be the only life-form to take any interest in me. I shook my head so that my favorite earrings jingled, the ones with the tiny shells that Dad had brought me from Greece.

If you closed your eyes and held your face up to the spring sun, you could almost believe you were somewhere else, in the south. . . . I could actually feel the first summer freckles of the year starting to sprout.

When I opened my eyes again, I noticed an old wooden footbridge that stretched across to the opposite side of the river in an arch. The bleached wooden boards bounced under my feet. Afraid they might suddenly give way, I looked down as I walked. That's why I only noticed the five guys when I was already halfway across the bridge. They were sitting on the railing, drinking beer and spitting into the flowing river. What I really wanted to do was turn around, but to run off at that point would have been cowardly. So I leaned on the railing with my back to them and lit a cigarette. I suppressed a sudden urge to cough as I exhaled smoke through my nose. Stay cool, Mia . . .

But I could sense that the guys were staring at me like they'd never seen a female before. There probably weren't a lot of girls around here in pale makeup with dark lines around their eyes and wearing black velvet clothes. This getup somehow made me feel confident, as if I were wearing a vampire costume that made me invincible. Who would dare approach such a monster bride? A dumb dog, at most, since most people look at the packaging first and not at what's inside. That's one of the basic principles of advertising psychology, a subject my father often teaches.

~~~~~

That day, my clothes didn't protect me. The boys' eyes were stuck to my body like spiderwebs. I wanted to shove the whole crew off the bridge and watch them flounder in the water like oversized insects. . . . But of course, I didn't do anything of the sort. Instead, I tried to ignore their stares. The sun reflected off the water, and I was a little bit dizzy.

"You're new here, aren't you?" one of the boys finally asked, interrupting the awkward silence. For better or worse, I had to turn around.

Aha! So this was the top dog among the natives. He didn't look half bad, actually: wiry, athletic build, and brown curls. I guessed he was about eighteen. He looked familiar somehow, there was something about his eyes . . . light blue eyes that suddenly twinkled in the sunlight. The same eyes as the old woman in the garden! Was that his grandmother?

"I think we're neighbors," he said. "My brother, Jay," he continued, nodding his chin in the direction of a lanky guy with light, shoulder-length hair who looked like he was about to fall off the railing, "and I saw you unloading the moving van this morning."

In the stillness that followed, we sized each other up. This was probably the part where I was supposed to introduce myself in a friendly way, tell them where I came from, and so forth. But I kept my mouth shut. I hadn't counted on his persistence.

"My name is Alex, by the way. Alex Stonebrook," he said, extending his hand toward me. I was so astonished by this old-fashioned gesture that I automatically responded in kind. His handshake was warm and firm. I let go of his hand quickly.

"And what's your name?"

This guy had way too much confidence. I blew cigarette smoke in his face but even that didn't faze him.

"Mmmm . . ." he hummed, sniffing, "Vanilla?"

When he smiled at me, tiny dimples appeared in his cheeks, the kind that make you want to touch them with your little finger. He was surely aware of that—a regular backwater Casanova. He probably expected all the girls to just fall into his arms when he pulled that stunt with the dimples. But if he thought I would fall for it, he was mistaken.

All of a sudden, rage welled up in me. I wanted to show him, the self-appointed king of the village, oh, yeah! I wanted to get a rise out of that calm face, wipe away that satisfaction with himself and his little world.

"Oh, so you know what that is around here? Vanilla?" Even to my own ears, my voice sounded too sharp, too sarcastic. He just laughed.

"Yeah, imagine that. There's more here than you probably think. If you like, I could show you a few things. You know where I live."

That was either the dumbest pick-up line I had ever heard, or the guy was just plain friendly. I didn't know what to make of it.

"We'll see," I mumbled, shrugging my shoulders, turning to go. I tried not to sway, but I was still dizzy. That must have been from the sun.

"Hey, I still don't know your name!" Alex called after me.

"Mia!" I called back over my shoulder. "I'm Mia." A light breeze lifted my hair, making my shell earrings jingle quietly. At the end of the bridge sat the stray dog, waiting for me. And suddenly it seemed to smell a little like spring, after all.

Chapter 2

Alexander

"Jay, we have to go! Where are you, you bum?" The wooden steps creaked in protest as I stormed down the stairs. No Jay in the entryway, no Jay in the kitchen. . . . I grabbed two apples from the fruit bowl in passing before I ran out into the yard.

I finally found him in back on our dock. I should have known, actually. The early fog still hung above the water as the sky slowly became lighter. And right in the middle of it, my brother. He crouched there with his head tilted to one side and rocked slightly on the balls of his feet. I have no idea what that's all about.

"Hey," I said. It seemed wrong that I was here, as if I had interrupted him while he was praying or something.

He finally seemed to notice me. He managed to stand up, stretched. "Hey, Skip," he said and smiled at me. Skip, my pirate name. Jay was the only one who still called me that. Only then did I notice that he had his voice recorder in his hand.

"Did you record something?"

"Yeah, do you want to hear it?" Eagerly he rewound and then pressed play. Amidst the white noise, if you listened carefully, you could just make out the twittering of birds.

"Birdspring, spring birds," Jay said with satisfaction.

He loved to play with words like that, turning them around, stretching them out, as if he had raspberry gum in his mouth that he was pushing around with his tongue. Like the sound of the words was more important to him than their meaning.

"Ah," I mumbled, pretending that I understood. In fact, the only thing I understood right then was that I should never have given him that stupid tape recorder for Christmas. Hopefully, it would never occur to him to play his spring birds recording to anyone at school. Because I had absolutely no desire to beat up Wolf or some other idiot just because he said aloud what everyone thought: my little brother was a nutcase.

"Come on, we're running late," I urged. "Here's your breakfast." Clumsily, Jay caught the apples I tossed to him.

"I've already eaten," he said but bit eagerly into one of the apples. "I've been up since six already. Not like you, sleepyhead!"

I punched him lightly in the side. "Yeah, well then hopefully you're in good shape for the Spanish test today. Did you look over the thing with the "if" sentences again?" No reply. He stubbornly fixed his gaze on the tennis shoes that compliantly carried him to school. I sighed. I thought so. He had probably just whiled away the time somewhere along the river again, maybe on the island where we always used to play in our tree house.

Between two bites of apple Jay finally mumbled, "You know I'm not interested in that stuff, Skip." Yeah, I knew that for sure. In fact, I believe that was the main difference between my brother and the rest of the world. Most people spend half of their day doing things that have to be done, even if they don't actually feel like doing them at all: going to the dentist, mowing the lawn, growing up . . . the things that are necessary to make your way through life.

Jay didn't do that. He didn't boycott to be defiant (although our father always insisted he did). That would never have occurred to him. It was just that those kinds of things weren't important to him.

"Grandma will kill you if you bring home another bad test grade! And me, too, because I didn't make sure you did better. So don't mess it up, Jay. Just try to pretend it's biology or something else that you like, okay? For me?"

Jay grinned his typical grin, with one eye, the blue one, laughing. But the other eye, the green-brown one, remained serious. His faraway, foreign eye.

Some people found Jay unsettling. In moments like this, I could understand that somehow, though I had seen his bi-colored eyes all my life and was used to them. "Look, there goes the new girl!" I said quickly.

Even from a hundred feet away you could see that this Mia was from the city. She shuffled along the road without looking to the left or the right. I felt compelled to stare at her all the time. I couldn't help myself. She wasn't even particularly sexy or anything. I had seen much prettier girls. I had already slept with much prettier girls.

But in spite of that, or maybe because of it, maybe it was this exotic . . . different-ness that captivated me. There was something about her that made her seem utterly out of place. It wasn't the black Goth clothes or the dyed-black hair, which made her face look sickly. It was something else . . .

I was only half listening to Jay, who was just saying ". . . in my class think Mia is an arrogant bitch because she doesn't really talk to anyone. And she's been here three weeks already!"

"And what do you think?" I asked.

"I think she's crazy!" Jay said, grinning. By then we had reached school. Just in time, because the bell was already ringing. Wolf, Matt, and the other guys were waiting for us.

"Hey, boys, having a little recording session again were you?" Wolf grinned, punching Jay a little too hard on the shoulder. "What was it this time, ducks quacking?"

"Shut up, idiot," I said in a dangerously quiet voice, and he did.

Only when I looked up again did I see that Mia had been watching us. She stood all by herself in the middle of the schoolyard and looked over at us, while she chewed on her fingernails. And then I suddenly figured out what I found so strange about her. Other people wore black because it was stylish or made them look thinner or because they just liked it, but Mia wore it like a widow, like someone in mourning. Who or what was she mourning?

When I nodded at her, she quickly looked away. What I really wanted to do was to go over to her and hold her jittery, raw hands in mine.

~~~~~

After the long, torturous hours of the school day, Jay and I finally sat at Grandma's dining room table again.

Above the table hung a singing fish. It was plastic and wore a Santa's hat. Dad found it last year at a Christmas market in the city, and the board from which it hung was nailed into the wall above the table. It was probably compensation for the fact that he still hadn't been able to snag Old George, a devious pike that lived under our dock. Twice already he had managed to get Old George on the hook, and twice he had seen nothing more than George's dorsal fin as he dove back down into the brown-green depths of the river.

Sometimes, when our father was in a good mood, he let the fish sing for us before we ate: "Jingle bells, jingle bells ..." The plastic fish clapped its mouth open and shut and swung its tail rhythmically in time to the canned microphone voice. My brother, our father, and I thought this was hilarious.

My grandmother less so; she saw the singing fish as a kind of blasphemy. In a respectable household, people should say a prayer before eating. Our grandmother was a strict Catholic. While my father sat on the dock fishing at 9:30 Sunday morning, trying one more time to reel in Old George, she was off to church. She would have liked to drag me and Jay with her, since she thought a little Christian guidance would be good for us. There were not many things

23

we had managed to establish against Grandma's will, but the church boycott and the singing fish were among them.

But today the singing fish remained quiet. Grandma said a prayer, with a slight suggestion of triumph in her voice, as she had the last word this time: "Come Lord Jesus and be our guest . . ."

"Amen," we murmured and then started eating. We could tell Dad was in a bad mood, not only because of the fish's silence, but also the way he ate. Usually he shoved his food thoughtfully onto his fork, chewed thoroughly, and rinsed it down with a sip of beer . . . everything at his own pace. Today, he just shoveled potatoes into his mouth without paying any attention.

Grandma noticed this, too, of course. "Trouble at work?"

"Hmmm," grumbled my father. "Not enough orders." Dully, he stared at the delicate fork in his large hand. He squeezed his fingers around it, and then loosened his grip again. You could seldom read anything from his facial expression, but his hands gave him away. This time I couldn't quite interpret the gesture. Maybe it was fear.

No wonder. If he lost his job in the carpentry workshop, he probably wouldn't find another job here, and then we'd have to move away. I couldn't imagine that. Grandma always said that our family had lived here so long that we had river water in our veins instead of blood. When it came to my father, she was right.

It was quiet at the table, just the sound of silverware clinking. The vegetables swelled in my mouth. They were overcooked and there was hardly any salt on the potatoes. Something like that would never have happened to Grandma before, but recently . . . Of course, I didn't say anything to anyone; we didn't want to offend her. I could just imagine how she would get huffy: "If my cooking doesn't suit you anymore, you can just cook for yourselves from now on!"

Grandma put another lightly burnt bratwurst on my father's plate, as if she wanted to cheer him up with it. "And how was your Spanish test? Did it go well?" Grandma asked in a forced cheerful voice, fixing her penetrating blue gaze on Jay.

If that was supposed to be an attempt to steer conversation toward a less touchy subject, it was definitely the wrong question. "Hmmm," Jay replied, quickly stuffing another potato in his mouth.

"Your grandmother asked you a question, young man," Dad said, giving Jay a shove. He, in turn, hit his water glass with his fork. Pling! The sound made Jay forget Grandma's question entirely. I could see it in the way he tilted his head to the side. He tapped his fork against the glass again, but very softly, and listened intently.

He drank a gulp and tried it again. This time the tone was brighter, clearer. We stared at him. Jay didn't notice. His eyes glistened with excitement as he continued the water concert.

I considered whether I should kick him hard in the shin to bring him to his senses again. "Stop that, boy." Dad didn't speak any louder than usual, but I could hear the tension of an impending storm in his voice. My glass was fuller, and the sound more of a clang: drrr . . . and again drrr . . .

Then Dad slammed his fist on the table so hard that water spilled onto the table. "Stop that!" he roared. It didn't happen often that he totally lost his cool. But when he did, it almost always had to do with my brother. My father had never understood him. Even I didn't always understand Jay, although I probably knew him better than anyone else in the world. But our father didn't even try.

"I will not allow my son to become a space cadet," he said, breathing heavily, and it sounded as if wanted to justify his outburst. Then he said more softly, "I won't tolerate him becoming like his mother . . ."

"Eric!" Grandma interrupted him. Her voice was as sharp as a kitchen knife.

The silence that followed hummed in my ears. Dad looked down at his hands as if he had never seen them before. They were shaking. Mine were trembling, too. I wished I could punch him, like I would Wolf or someone else. I wished our mother were here. I wished . . .

While we still sat there like manikins, Grandma took control of the situation again. After she had admonished our father, she then turned to Jay, who was absently staring out the window.

"And you will stop playing around during the meal, which your father worked hard to provide! You are grounded for the night!" Jay stood up, without saying a word, and shuffled to the door with his plate. I also stood up.

"You two always stick together, huh?" my father asked behind me. I turned around again, my hand already on the doorknob. I looked him straight in the eyes and hoped that he would notice—notice that I despised him at that moment and that I swore to myself I would never be like him.

Maybe he did get it. He pushed his chair back abruptly, but as he crossed the room to the porch door, I saw that his arms were hanging down as if his hands had suddenly become too heavy for him. "I have to get back to work. Might be late tonight, Iris," I heard him say to Grandma before he stepped out into the yard.

Only the singing fish was left behind in the dining room—keeping Grandma company as she ate her vegetables in stoic silence.

~~~~~

I went up to my room. After that meal, I felt beat. This horror family really got to me. I wanted to get out of here.

The globe stood on my desk. When I turned it on, the globe's oceans lit up in blue and, embedded in them, the continents in golden yellow, brown, and green. I had marked all the places my mom had sent me pictures of with red sticker dots. Over the years, they had added up.

Time for a little adventure trip. How long had it been since I had done that? Six months, maybe longer? I gave the globe a push and it began to spin on its axis. Faster and faster, the colored dots flew by. Ready, set . . . I closed my eyes and touched the globe with my index finger. The red dot closest to my finger was Mindanao. Of all places.

Mindanao is an island near the Philippines. That's the place the shell came from—on my seventh birthday—the first place she went after she left us.

I rifled through the cardboard carton under my bed for the envelope of photos from her first report. Because I didn't have enough room on my walls, I could only hang up the most recent ones.

There they were. I leafed through them. There weren't any pictures of my mother among them. She only photographed other people, landscapes, animals: a man splitting a papaya with a machete, the glistening of the machete and his white teeth; a spotted snake gliding along the forest floor; the sea, gleaming turquoise blue. The colors seemed to hover in the air above the bay. That was it; that was the photo I wanted to travel with today. One of my favorite pictures, it had always faithfully led me to my destination.

I threw myself on the bed. With one hand, I held the photo in front of my face, and with the other, I pressed the conch shell to my ear. Its weight was heavy and good in my hand. The celluloid sea began to roar.

I tried to imagine I was sitting on that beach, digging my toes into the hot sand. How the air tasted! Like algae and salt. And the wind was spraying foam into my face so that even my lips tasted salty, and later in the evening, at home, I'd find tiny grains of sand in my clothes.

I had never actually been to the sea. We didn't have money to travel.

Concentrate now! I gathered my thoughts—ocean, space. I sat on the beach, the waves crashing. Back there at the edge of the picture, where the cliffs were, a figure appeared. It was a woman with long blonde hair wearing a white sundress. She ran right along the water's edge, where the waves break over your ankles and you can feel their pull as they withdraw back into the ocean.

The woman was my mother.

Soon, she would sit down next to me and ask, "How are you doing, Skip?" We would sit in the sand and just talk. About little things. Or just watch this glittering, endlessly moving water together.

I heaved an exasperated sigh. It just didn't work! Had I forgotten how to do it by now? Maybe it was better that way. Grandma always said that you should keep both feet on the ground. I thought so, too. But then why did I feel so . . . crap!

My mother's face was a blurred fleck. When I tried to fill in her features, it was always just the immortalized facial features from the old black-and-white pictures that hung all over our house. The little personal gestures that everyone has were gone. Forgotten.

Only one image remained: *my mother stood knee deep in the river and stretched out both of her hands toward me.*

Wolf once asked me if I hated her. I told him no, and that was true. I could understand that she didn't want to stay here, in this little town, with this man. The only thing I didn't understand was why she hadn't taken Jay and me with her.

I used to hope that no packet of photographs would arrive for my birthday; that instead, she would be standing at the door again, coming to pick us up.

It was strange that Jay had never seemed to miss her. I had never seen him cry, and he had never asked about her, either. But he was a lot younger than I was when she took off. He was only five. I was almost seven then.

And besides, he had me. I looked after him. Always had.

Damn it! I wasn't one of those sissies who cried himself to sleep because his mama had up and left. But sometimes . . .

"Come," I whispered into the sound of the waves, "please come!"

Chapter 3

Jay

Grounded again! And just because of that stupid Spanish test. Grandma had studied the D on my paper for a long time, as if she could turn it into a B with the power of her gaze, and then growled: "This week you will not set foot outside your room after you get home from school, is that understood? You should spend some time seriously thinking about what you need to change in your life."

I liked my life exactly the way it was, and I told her so, too. She just snorted. "I'll make your life a living nightmare if you don't learn that Spanish grammar inside and out!"

So there I sat, chewing on my pencil and looking outside at the rain. "Susan would write a letter if . . ."

I asked myself who this faceless Susan would write a letter to. She should write my brother a letter. He loved letters and photos.

Maybe Susan was writing to her mother . . .

Why weren't those things ever in the Spanish books? They just left out the most important things!

"Susan would write a . . ."

The water gurgled in the gutters while I watched the path of the drops rolling down my windowpane and joining to form little rivulets, then streams . . .

I had never been able to resist rainy days at the river. Besides, Alina was sure to be waiting for me already. Hopefully, she wasn't mad because I didn't come yesterday. And the day before yesterday. Or the day before that, either . . .

"Susan would . . ." Oh, to hell with this Susan! Alina was waiting.

Quickly, I slipped into my rain gear and snuck down the stairs in my socks, rubber boots in my hand. Chrr, chrr went the steps, like sleeping dogs. I had to skip the fifth one from the top or it would wake up and bark.

I was already halfway down when a door opened upstairs. Skip always heard me. I guess that's the way it is with big brothers. He looked down at me and then whispered, "Be careful not to fall in the river!"

Even though he was grinning, I could hear the concern in his voice. He always worried too much, even though I could swim better than him. Skip didn't like the river.

"No need to worry, Skip, I can take perfectly good care of myself," I said quietly. He muttered something and closed the door again.

Outside, the rain sang with a thousand voices. *Drip, drip* . . . it whispered in the new leaves, telling them stories of its travels. Just like spelling words into the hands of a blind person. The trees sighed then and were happy. I could hear it.

With squelching rubber boots, I ran across the wet grass, so fast that I almost fell. I didn't look over at the neighbor's yard. And what was more important, I didn't listen in that direction, either. No.

But I couldn't stop myself from thinking about it: how I happened to be passing her house, the house of the crazy girl. And then I heard it, that sound, that sound that wrapped itself around my ankle like twine and pulled me over the fence. I couldn't do anything else, I had to follow it. It sounded like a violin or something, but deeper, fuller.

Every stroke of the bow sank into my flesh, vibrated in my bones. How incredible that crazy girl could produce such sounds!

And then I stood under the window, beneath the cherry tree that blossomed whiter than white. I just stood there and listened. The sounds fell like cherry blossoms on my face, cool and soft. It was like snow and spring at the same time.

My heart contracted. Maybe it was fear, maybe something else I'd never experienced before that moment. I thought I would die. And I thought that I wouldn't even mind, as long as the music continued.

I have no idea how long it lasted. At some point, the music stopped. I didn't die. Instead, I went home.

That had been three days ago. I hadn't told anyone about it, not Skip, not even Alina, and I told her everything. But that . . . *that* I wanted to keep for myself, somehow. Just for me.

≈≈≈≈≈

I could already see Alina on the dock from a distance. She was waiting for me, even if she acted as if she just happened to be standing there because she felt like it right then. A slender shadow in the rain. Her long hair, her clothes, everything dripped with moisture, but she didn't seem to be cold.

"Hello," I lowered my voice involuntarily as I greeted her and was afraid she'd notice. That she could hear the new sound . . . deep within me. It might make her sad. Or furious.

Her face was serious as she turned to me, and she squinted her eyes. Raindrops hung from her eyelashes. "I thought you had forgotten me." Every word was a pebble that stroked the water's surface and then sank into the unfathomed depths.

"I was grounded," I said, trying to convince myself it wasn't a lie. We were quiet for a while and watched the seething river.

"Promise me," Alina finally exclaimed. Her voice sounded like a willow rod then, lashing, hard. "Promise me that you'll never forget me!"

I spit into my hand and swore like I had always promised her, even as a kid: "I'll never, ever forget you!"

For a moment, she looked me over—scrutinized me. Then she smiled and climbed into the boat that was tied to the dock. "Come on!"

Our boat, the *Bounty*, was in desperate need of a new coat of paint. It had seen better times, back when my brother had still been Skipper, and we waged battles against the South Sea pirates with the other guys. Or fed the Nile crocodiles with wretched mutineers. It all depended on what books Skip had been reading, or where the last letters had come from.

The players changed; Matt and Wolf were often with us back then. But my brother was always in charge of the boat, the Skipper. And I was his exploration officer.

At some point, Skip became Alex. For everyone, except me.

Now he rarely used the *Bounty*. And never for adventure trips on the Nile. He didn't like the river anymore.

So I had inherited the boat. I took it out often to meet Alina on the island. She sat opposite me, looking in the direction we were traveling, trailing a hand in the water and humming contentedly while I rowed. I put power into the oars and pulled all the way through. After a few strokes, I had found my rhythm. It was a good feeling to have perfect timing and to dip the oars so that they hardly splashed at all. The boat glided through the water like an arrow. On the surface were countless circles that ran together and became part of the river again, like tiny explosions. The river seemed to boil. All around us the rain pattered, tapped, drummed, rustled, murmured. And we were in the midst of it with our boat. I slapped the oars on the surface a few times, hard, so the water sprayed, and imagined we were the kettledrums in this orchestra.

"Do it again!" Alina laughed.

But even that couldn't silence it, that sound that still resonated in me. For three days already. It penetrated the water concert like a sudden beam of light on a rainy day.

The sun fought its way in front of the clouds and made the world fragment into a thousand drops. A kingfisher flew above the river, a flapping blue streak. The island appeared in front of us.

~~~~~

The weather cleared up, and the sky turned blue as I came home again. Lights were on in the kitchen, winking at me invitingly through the twilight. I peered through the window to scout out the situation.

Uh, oh, there would be trouble! Apparently, I had already missed dinner. There was Skip, helping Grandma with the dishes. He washed. She dried.

It was strange to watch them . . . my family . . . without me. Alone with my brother, Grandma allowed herself to look older. In the yellow glow of the kitchen light, she seemed almost as fragile as the porcelain plates she dried, carefully, each with the same spare motions.

She was saying something to my brother; I saw her mouth open and close approvingly. Although I couldn't hear the words, I understood her meaning: *good boy*.

Grandma never said anything like that to me. I was "chaos personified," a "stray dog," a "daydreamer. Like your mother." Configurations of letters that didn't touch me. Words, just words. The only bad part was *how* she said them. They sounded like mortal sins, while her lips became a line as thin as a pencil.

I leaned my forehead on the cool pane of glass and felt the vibration of Grandma's words in my head: *good boy, good boy*.

But Skip didn't hear it at all, I think, even though he was standing right next to her. I watched him. His hands dutifully scrubbed the dishes, one glass after the other. His glance moved in my direction, but his eyes didn't see me. Even though I was standing only a few steps from the window, they saw right through me, through the river lying in the twilight and our town behind it . . . at something far, far away from here.

He always had that expression on his face when he looked at the photographs.

He only came to when Grandma spoke to him again. Slowly, like a swimmer surfacing out of deep water. He smiled, nodded an answer, and then his face fell as he noticed me standing at the window.

Unfortunately, Grandma discovered me, too. She tore open the kitchen window. The light carved deep folds in her face, like in the antiquated woodcut of two praying hands that hung over her bed. Yellow light fell on my face and blinded me.

". . . sneaking around the house like a thief . . ." Grandma scolded. "Come inside this instant, Jay!" Resistance was futile. Crouched on a stool in the kitchen, I let Grandma rub my hair dry with a kitchen towel while Skip slipped away, grinning.

"You could have caught your death outside in the rain . . . would have served you right! You've been out on the river again, haven't you? How often have I told you that you shouldn't go there, that it's dangerous?"

I thought about it briefly. "At least three times this week," I said, and raised my shoulders, ducking another round of her tirade.

But Grandma just shook her head and grumbled, "The apple doesn't fall far from the tree!" Then she asked, "Were you at least wearing your chain?"

I nodded and pulled the narrow silver chain with the cross hanging from it out of the collar of my shirt. Grandma touched the tiny Jesus with a finger. "Our savior certainly has his hands full protecting you," she sighed.

She sounded tired, and somehow that sound was worse than her angry voice. "Go get washed, Jay, you've got dirt on your face." She stroked my cheek with her worn-out hand and murmured, "What on earth am I supposed to do with you, child?"

I studied my own hands with the dirty bands under the fingernails and didn't have an answer for her.

Chapter 4

Mia

||||||||||||||||||||||||||||||||||||||||||||||||||||||||||||||||||||||||||||||||||||||||||||||||||||||||||||||||||||||||

We ran out of chocolate-covered raisins. That's why I was on my way to that tiny excuse of a grocery story instead of sitting at my observation post at the window.

≈ ≈ ≈ ≈ ≈

I didn't like to admit it, but in the past few weeks observing the neighbors' house had become almost a compulsion, like watching one of those soap operas that you absolutely have to see the next episode of. Except it was so much more boring. And at the same time much more interesting . . .

When people were actually out in the yard, I couldn't even understand what they were talking about. Nothing more spectacular happened than Alex watering the flowers, or his brother setting off toward the river occasionally. Nonetheless—or maybe because of it—I was glued to the window. I put words in their mouths and untamable, dangerous passions in their hearts. I wrote the screenplay of their destinies: The grandmother was having an affair with the mailman; the boys' mother—a person who might have played that role in real life hadn't been spotted over there so far—had filed for divorce because her husband was an alcoholic.

A hundred times I had sworn to myself I would stop it. But I just couldn't let it go, couldn't stop thinking what might be going on in their heads, filling out the contours of the family life that was playing out no more than three hundred feet away from me and yet was completely different from mine.

~~~~~

The stray dog, which was already waiting for me at the bridge, trotted along behind me when I came by on my chocolate-covered raisin mission. I shouldn't have fed it the other day; now I'd always have this mutt hanging on my heels.

"Don't you have anything better to do than to follow me?" I asked, and stood still. The dog stopped in its tracks. It eyed me attentively from a distance and wiggled its left ear.

"You don't belong to anyone, do you? No one wants to have you?" I continued, in a nasty mood due to prolonged chocolate withdrawal. "No wonder, you're certainly nothing to look at!"

"Wuff," the dog replied defiantly, as if to say "You, too!"

I continued. Occasionally, I turned around to see if the stupid dog was still following me. It was. That made me happy, somehow. Silly, I know, but I felt like we had something in common. If nothing else, we both liked chocolate-covered raisins.

When I got to the store, the distance between us had shrunk to a few feet. "Wait here, dog," I said. My hairy companion yawned, as if to let me know, maybe I'll do it but maybe not. Depends on whether or not I feel like it.

As I stood in the checkout line, I saw it still sitting outside at the curb.

With three packages of chocolate-covered raisins in my pockets, I left the store—and almost ran into her. The grandmother! She wore one of her inevitable housecoats, shuffling along the street with her cane in one hand and a giant shopping bag in the other.

It was a surreal sensation, as if you suddenly bumped into someone who only exists in your imagination and not in your run-of-the-mill, ordinary life. Sort of like running into Johnny Depp in a jogging suit at the gas station.

While I was still staring after her with a mixture of shame and fascination, one of the handles of her plastic shopping bag suddenly tore. Rice spilled over the sidewalk. A milk container burst and streams of white trickled over the asphalt. Vegetables tumbled every which way; a pepper rolled almost to my feet.

The dog made the best of this opportunity and took off with a bag of sausages in its mouth. "Hey, dog! Drop it!" I yelled after it. Of course, it didn't listen.

The grandmother didn't curse, like any normal person might have done. She bent over to gather her things, a gnarled branch bending. I thought I heard a brittle crackling and could already imagine the headlines: *Old Woman*

Breaks in Two While Gathering Vegetables—Teenager Watches Without Lifting a Finger.

There wasn't anyone on the street except me. I guess there was no way around doing my duty as a citizen, my good deed for the day. On my knees, I chased rolling peppers, and I must have picked up a hundred little teabags off the ground.

"Um . . . here," I said, the pockets of my jacket stuffed with carrots and my arms full of yogurt containers. Unfortunately, the old woman didn't make a move to take the things from me.

"Should I help you carry everything home?" I asked reluctantly. I had no desire to meet her, let alone to carry her shopping bags. I wanted to continue observing her from the safe distance of my room. But if I hadn't asked, I would have felt like a socially impaired idiot the rest of the day and that would have been even worse.

Her blue eyes bored into mine, taking in my baggy velvet pants, the big earrings, my carefully made-up face with dark eyelids. I was sweating and had the feeling my makeup might melt away under her gaze.

"You're the girl from next door, aren't you?"

"Hmmm," I answered.

The grandmother snorted and made a movement with her head that you might interpret as a nod. "Then we're going the same way anyhow!" With those words, she hobbled away with her tapping cane. I panted behind her.

The way home had never seemed so long. We didn't exchange a single word the entire way. When we finally arrived, I was so exhausted that I hardly noticed the dark

42

entry hall we passed through when we stepped into the house. I just had vague impressions of photographs, lots and lots of large photographs of animals, with close-ups of dragonflies, beetles, and other creepy, crawly things.

I stumbled into a kitchen, where I helped the old woman put away the mountain of groceries in an ancient refrigerator. "Now I'll make us both a cold drink. . . . What's your name, young lady?"

"Mia."

"Iris Wagner." Her handshake was astonishingly strong. "You can call me Iris. Go sit down in the living room," the old woman ordered. As I left the kitchen, I could hear her mumbling to herself, "Mia, how can anyone name their child such a thing."

Alone in the living room, my eyes immediately scanned the room with curiosity: typical boring, flowery wallpaper, furniture with chipped edges. Everything seemed used, but neat and orderly. Above the table hung a cross—and next to it a plastic fish!

I didn't know exactly how I had imagined the inside of the house, but certainly not like this. It was more eccentric and much more lived in than in my soap opera fantasy. More real, with all the knickknacks and cactuses on the windowsills. It wasn't scenery for a play, but a house, where real people lived.

A family photo on the wall caught my attention. It was one of those posed studio pictures, with everyone smiling tensely at the camera, and featured a couple with two children.

The man I recognized as a younger, good-looking version of Mr. Stonebrook. He stood behind a young woman—a girl—with long, light hair, and he had a smile on his face that seemed to alternate between pride and bashfulness. The toddler sitting on the woman's lap I recognized right away because of the two different-colored eyes. The older boy stood next to them with his hand on his mother's arm. His expression was oddly serious, much too grown up for a child. Alex.

But it was the woman whose look touched me somehow. Maybe because she seemed to still be so young, hardly older than me. It was weird to imagine already being a mother. But what was it. . . . I stepped closer to the picture. A tiny, hidden smile played around the corners of her mouth that didn't seem to fit with her good wife and mother role, as if she wanted to toss back her long hair and laugh in the photographer's face mockingly because he didn't understand a thing. Or as if she just wanted to jump and get out of that faded photograph . . .

By then my face was so close to the picture that my nose was almost touching it. All at once, I was 100 percent sure: this woman had a secret. Her eyes, there was something strange about her eyes . . .

Shuffling steps. Startled, I jumped back. Iris Wagner came into the room with a tray on which two glasses slid back and forth.

"I was just looking at the picture," I said quickly.

"I saw that," she noted dryly.

"I'm sorry," I stuttered, suppressing the impulse to chew on my fingernails. "I didn't mean to be impolite, but . . ."

Unable to control my curiosity any longer, I pointed to the young woman in the photo. "Who is that?"

"My daughter, Katarina."

"She's very pretty."

"Yes. Pretty, and not quite right in the head," the old woman huffed, and set down the tray so hard that the glasses clattered. "Iced tea?"

I didn't dare say no. With a big gulp, I tried to swallow my questions: *Where is she now? Why did she go away and leave her kids here?*

With a quiet groan, Iris sat down on a stool across from me. She sipped at her glass (which definitely didn't contain iced tea but some other liquid that smelled suspiciously like brandy). And then—I couldn't believe my luck—she continued talking without any prompting.

"Did you see the pictures in the front hall? She wanted to be a photographer, Katarina. Tsk, tsk, such wild notions. She didn't get that from me! My husband and I finally convinced her to first get some training at the photo studio in the next town over. Something practical! But it didn't amount to anything." She shook her head and drained her glass. "Katarina even gave the other apprentice girl ideas with her fantastic tales. Before long, Ruth was just as crazy as she was. Faraway countries the two of them wanted to visit, get to know how people live there. 'As soon as I'm eighteen, I'm out of here!' Katarina always said."

I was liking this Katarina more and more.

"And did she make it? Did she live her dreams? Where is she now?" I asked eagerly.

45

With a sudden jerk, Iris set down her empty glass on the tray—as if she were trying to shake herself awake from a half-forgotten dream. Then she stood up, with some difficulty.

"Enough words wasted on days gone by," she murmured. "Now I really have to start making dinner. My men will be hungry when they come home."

I followed her into the kitchen. "Please, continue your story. It's really interesting."

"Really?" She studied me for a long while. Her eyes weren't unfriendly. "Well, if you're going to stand around you can help me peel the potatoes. We're having vegetable soup today."

I stared at the vegetable peeler she put in my hand. Until then, my culinary abilities had been limited to baking a frozen pizza.

"What are you waiting for? Get started!"

So I did. Astonishingly, I found that it was actually fun. As the smell of frying onions and bacon wafted to my nose, I even felt genuinely hungry for the first time in weeks.

"Of course, everything always turns out completely different than what you think, young lady," Iris said gruffly as she chopped her third potato already (I was still struggling with my first). "And so it was for Katarina. Because one day . . ." She stopped abruptly. "Hello you two lazybones, you're just in time!"

Her grandsons stood in the doorway with their eyes nearly popping out of their heads when they saw me standing in the kitchen. "Stop staring at my guest! It's rude!"

Iris snapped as her eyebrows shot up menacingly. The boys immediately looked in a different direction.

I suppressed a giggle; it was clear who was in charge here!

"Don't just stand there like a bump on a log, Jay, go set the table," Iris turned on the lanky guy with the uncanny eyes, who immediately slipped away. Then she handed her peeling knife to the astonished Alex. "Here, make yourself useful. I still need to get parsley from the garden."

As soon as she had turned her back on him, Alex lifted his eyebrows and crumpled his face in an expert parody of his grandmother. And when he started fumbling around with a carrot just like she must always do with her cane, I almost burst out laughing.

But only almost. *Pull yourself together, Mia!* I quickly bent over my cutting board so my hair covered my face. Through the protective curtain, I glanced over at Alex, who held two carrots to his mouth like orange fangs: *she's a real dragon.*

Then he shrugged his shoulders and graced me with his widest grin.

I didn't smile back, just fixed my eyes firmly on the work in front of me. But it didn't help. Alex seemed to fill the room completely with his energy, his good mood.

I wish I could be like that! I suddenly thought. *I wish it were that simple!* And just like that, the kitchen seemed to be much too small for both of us. We stood so close to each other at the counter that I imagined I could feel the heat from his body. Much too close.

47

It was hot. My hands trembled. I chopped into the potato, hacking it into tiny slices. And the whole time I could feel him watching me.

"I haven't seen you smile yet. Why don't you ever laugh?" Alex suddenly asked.

Then I cut into my finger.

"Uh oh, you cut yourself," he said. My hand was in his, no idea how that happened so quickly. "Let's see." He bent over my hand.

Suddenly, I thought of a scene I had observed at school a while ago: Alex defending his little brother against some guy who had made fun of Jay. The other guy was at least two heads taller than Alex. If only I had had someone looking out for me.

"The cut isn't deep, but you should still put a bandage on it," Alex said.

I saw my blood dripping onto the floor. Red, very red against the white tiles. And then I knew: he might become dangerous to me! Nicolas, Nicolas . . . droned through my head.

"It's okay." I pulled my hand away from Alex so forcefully that he looked at me in surprise. I sucked on my finger as if I wanted to hide the cut.

Everything was swirling around in my head. All I wanted was to get away. "I think . . . I think I'd better go now," I said.

"But wait, don't you want to stay and eat with us?" Alex asked, irritated. "After all, you helped cook." But I was already on my way to the door.

"No, my parents are probably waiting for me." At least I still knew how to lie.

"Well at least say good-bye to my grandma. She'll be disappointed if you just leave."

This guy didn't give up so quickly. And then he asked, "Why do you always run away, anyhow?"

Caught in the act.

I didn't know how to respond. Attack is the best defense, so I said the first thing that occurred to me. To my own surprise, I even meant it seriously: "Your grandmother shouldn't go shopping alone anymore." My voice sounded more forceful than I had intended. More involved.

Alex's face suddenly became a closed book, and I saw that I had instinctively said just the right thing to put him off.

"We manage just fine," he said, suddenly reserved.

"Sorry, it's none of my business, but . . ."

"You're right," Alex interrupted, holding the door open for me. "It's none of your business!" My attempt to flee had turned into being thrown out. I felt a sense of bitter triumph as I left the Stonebrooks' house. Behind me, the door slammed shut.

It was better this way. That was dangerous territory. But then why was I so disappointed?

A small, stupid part of me hoped Alex would call me back. But no one called, so I slowly made my way down to the garden gate. And then I noticed them for the first time: prints of bare, wet feet that led all over the paved garden path and got lost between the rose beds.

I put my own foot next to one of them. The prints were made by feet even smaller than mine, so it couldn't be anyone from the neighboring house. Everyone in the family was quite tall. Apparently, someone was prowling around the Stonebrooks' house who didn't have any business being there. Someone was watching them . . . just like me. How strange that I had never noticed anything suspicious from my post at the window.

I felt a cold prickling sensation on the back of my neck as I stared at the footprints slowly fading away in the evening sunlight. They disappeared as if they had never existed at all.

Maybe I should warn the Stonebrooks that someone was sneaking around their house? I glanced at the closed front door. No, I and my opinions were not welcome there. It was none of my business what problems these people had. I had enough of my own.

Nicolas's name still droned in my head as I quickly ran down the garden path.

≈≈≈≈≈

"Careful, it's fresh out of the oven!" my mother warned as she set the casserole down on our dining room table. In the dish was a brown-green mass that she described, with great pride, as herbed leek soufflé. "Hopefully your dad will be home soon," Mother said, looking impatiently at the clock. "It has to be eaten while it's hot, before it collapses."

Since we had been living here, my mother spent a lot of time in the kitchen, where she funneled her ambition into trying out exotic recipes "for the next time we have guests over again."

I knew she was feeling lonely. One time I happened to overhear her talking on the phone with one of her friends in the city. "This is the most backward place you could imagine!" she complained into the phone. "But the worst of it is the people! They're like a secret society; as the new person in town I feel like a total outsider." Her friend apparently said something, because my mother was quiet for a moment. Then she laughed a bitter laugh: "My husband? Mark always has so much to do and only comes home late. No sign of having more time for the family, and I can't reach Mia at all anymore. She's changed so much in the past year. She's so secretive and always wearing those awful black clothes."

I had been standing on the landing of the stairs and listening so hard that my insides were tied in knots, as if I were wearing a hard shell under my skin that was getting tighter and tighter around my heart. But now it was too late to break it open, too late . . . because I didn't know how anymore.

My mother had whispered into the phone, it sounded like a sob, but I didn't want to think about that: "Erica, I don't know what to do . . ."

I hurried up the stairs and tried to ignore the desperation in her voice. It sounded too much like mine.

~~~~~

Tick-tock went our antique grandfather clock. The soufflé had collapsed. While I poked around in the pathetic pile on my plate, I looked around our lovely new dining room. The evening sun fell through the carefully chosen draperies and shone on the old cherry-wood furniture. It was my mother's pride and joy. Before, she had always complained that they couldn't be appreciated in our old apartment.

Now her dream of a house in the country had come true—but looking at her tense expression as she stared at the clock, it didn't seem to mean much anymore. Dad's dinner was cold by now. And he hadn't missed much. I had only eaten a little of it for my mom's sake. I couldn't do any more for her. I couldn't help her any more than she could help me.

"I'll go up to my room," I said quietly. My mother just nodded.

Then I sat upstairs at the window again in my darkened room and looked over at the Stonebrooks' illuminated house and finally satisfied my craving for chocolate-covered raisins. Downstairs I heard the door opening, then the murmuring of voices.

As they slowly grew louder, like the muted, threatening buzzing of hornets, the lights of the neighbors' house swam before my eyes. Now I knew why I was always looking over there: because it was less real than things here.

Chapter 5

Alexander

||||||||||||||||||||||||||||||||||||||||||||||||||||||||||||||||||||||||||||||||||||||||||||||||||||||||||||||||||||||||||||||

So, I've been wanting to ask you. . . . Uh, would you maybe like to . . . ?

No, not like that. That would never work. It's always a bad idea to think too much in advance about something. That just pulls you down. I've tried it myself. So I didn't think for long about whether or not I should talk to her. I just did it and waited to see what would happen.

~~~~~

I met Mia on the way home. As always, she was wearing black clothes and had her arms crossed over her chest as if she were freezing. But it was already the end of May.

"Hi," I said casually, catching up with her. "Haven't seen you in a while." And it was true: since our train wreck of a conversation two weeks ago, we hadn't exchanged a single word.

"Hi, Alex." Her voice sounded hesitant. Cautious. No wonder, after I practically threw her out the last time we talked.

But that was before Grandma had collapsed on the way to the bakery. "Overexertion," the doctor had said, prescribing her some pills. "Quack," Grandma said, and didn't take them.

I sighed inwardly. It was probably best to get it over with. "You were right about what you said recently," I said without any introduction, "that my grandmother shouldn't go shopping by herself anymore."

"Yeah," Mia nodded, and just kept walking. Did she expect me to get on my knees and beg for forgiveness? Okay, I made a mistake. I'd just admitted it, hadn't I?

"It's just that I don't have so much time to take care of her," I explained as I tried to keep pace with her. "Next week our swimming pool opens again for the summer. I always work there part-time, save little kids from drowning and stuff like that."

She didn't seem the least bit impressed. "And why does that concern me, superhero?" she asked.

Ouch, that hit home. "Well, that's why I'm looking for someone who can help look out for Grandma. Just a couple of hours a week, you know, go shopping with her, help in the garden, keep her company." *Convince her to take her pills after all.* "And you got along with her so well." I tried to flatter Mia's vanity.

"You mean that kind of stuff is women's work, right?" Her voice dripped with sarcasm. Apparently, Mia had misunderstood my compliment, because she stepped up her pace, forcing me to practically jog along next to her.

"Yeah . . . no . . . " I didn't know what to say, and that almost never happens. "I only meant that she likes you. And my grandmother doesn't like a lot of people, believe me." I stood still. The whole thing was too dumb. Did I really need to run after this bitch and beg her to take the job? No, absolutely not!

My father was right, problems should stay in the family; we shouldn't involve any outsiders who didn't have any idea what was going on in the first place. The only trouble was that I didn't have the slightest idea how we could get everything under control by ourselves. Didn't matter.

"Just forget it!" I sniffed, and headed off in the opposite direction.

"Hey, wait a minute!"

I turned around. Mia stood a little way off and tugged on her hair. She suddenly seemed self-conscious. "I didn't say I didn't want to do it, did I?"

Can anyone understand women?

"So you do want the job?" I asked skeptically. "I can't pay you all that much." She studied me with that unfathomable expression. I had no idea what she wanted all of a sudden, but she certainly wasn't doing it for the money.

"I don't want any money," she said. "When should I start?"

~~~~~

The scent of suntan lotion on bare skin blended with the slightly stagnant smell of river water. You might almost think you were somewhere in Florida, where alligators sunned themselves in the canals of the Everglade swamps.

The frying oil sizzled. The detested smell of freshly cooked French fries rose to my nose and settled over the white beaches and everything else. I stood behind the deep fryer of the snack bar, sweating like a beast in the fields. Outside, the May sunshine beat down from the sky. It was the first truly hot day of the year, and the pool was correspondingly full.

Our swimming pool was old-fashioned in every way. The pool itself had been built in the 1920s and was filled by an inlet of the river. Even the changing rooms were from a different era. They were made of wood and had quite a few holes—most of them eagerly made with pocketknives so boys could watch girls as they changed. I could still remember my own excitement as I pressed my face against the warm, bleached wood, the feeling of doing something wonderfully forbidden as I peered through the narrow gap. Back then, girls seemed like creatures from another planet, mysterious and untouchable. Actually, not much has changed in that respect.

~~~~~

The day dragged on. Kids shrieked. Occasionally, they were reprimanded by their mothers, who lay on beach towels sunning themselves and chatting with their girlfriends. The shade of the trees moved across the trampled grass; soon it would be a complete wasteland.

From my spot at the snack bar, I had a good view of the diving boards. I watched the twelve-year-old boys endlessly doing pikes and flips from the high dive, or at least trying to. I could vaguely remember what it felt like when the days still stretched out before us, free and endless, and we had nothing better to do than to practice diving with our friends.

"Hey, Alex. Do you still have chocolate ice cream?" My buddy Wolf sauntered up to the counter with a wide grin on his face. "What's up, man? Enjoying the beautiful day?"

I muttered something incomprehensible and slammed his ice cream onto the counter. "You're much too aggressive, Alex. I think you urgently need a different job," Wolf suggested. Unfortunately, he seemed to be in a very talkative mood today. "So tell me, what're you going to do when you're done with school?" he asked as he ate his ice cream with obvious pleasure.

"Don't know exactly," I mumbled, and started scrubbing the countertop. "Community college, maybe. Or find some job or training program."

"I always thought you wanted to get out of here. Go on big trips. That's what you used to talk about all the time."

Yeah, I used to talk about wanting to go to sea practically every minute of every day. I was twelve years old. Everything seemed so simple to me back then.

"And I still want to!" I yelled at Wolf. "But it isn't that easy, get it?" It would have been too much to explain to him about Jay and Grandma—that I *couldn't* leave—because if I did, my family would fall apart.

"Man, are you on edge today!" Wolf threw a few coins on the counter. "Here. When you've got yourself under control again, come down to the bridge for a beer later." Then he took off.

≈≈≈≈≈

I hated the stench of oily French fries that clung to me after work. When my shift was finally over, I jumped from the high dive and hoped for the feeling it used to give me. But it wasn't there, not a trace of it.

Then I swam a few laps freestyle. But even the water couldn't wash away the smell of stale frying oil that had attached itself to my skin.

When I got home, I found Grandma and Mia in the garden. Mia came to our house often now, almost every day. Since then, the seasoning of our food had improved considerably. Grandma's mood, too.

At the moment, they were planting green beans. That is, Mia was planting the beans while Grandma sat on her old kitchen chair and talked—she was probably giving orders. They both looked rather content.

I was about to call to them and say hello when this stupid thought occurred to me: I wondered what they talked about when they were by themselves. Quietly, I ducked behind a blackberry hedge—and shrank back in disgust. In the thorns hung a fish skeleton. The sun-bleached bones were still complete, and the half-rotted head stared at me with sunken eyes. The rancid, nauseating stench of dead fish filled my nose. My God, that was disgusting! I tried to breathe through my mouth so I could concentrate on Mia and Grandma again.

It was a little like peering into those changing cabins as a kid. I could feel the hairs on my arms lifting. Because what

I heard was something I definitely didn't want to hear. But it was too late.

" . . . And then she met Eric," Grandma was telling her. "He was good looking back then, with a big, wide smile. And broad shoulders to lean on. He radiated a calm that Katarina never had. It was like she was born without it, like some other children are born with a finger or a toe too few. But Eric never saw her restlessness as a fault. He told me once that he felt alive when he was with my daughter." Deep in thought Grandma added, "It was as if they each had something the other was missing . . ."

"And what happened then?" Mia asked as she continued to dig energetically, her eyes trained on Grandma. The hole for the next plant was already so deep it looked like she wanted to dig her way to China.

"Things happened the way they had to. One morning, I found Katarina in the bathroom bent over the toilet getting sick. When she saw me she cried: 'Mama, what should I do?' I was flabbergasted. My sixteen-year-old daughter had gotten herself pregnant. 'You'll get married, of course,' I told her when I could speak again and had pushed the damp hair off her face. 'You're lucky that your Eric is a respectable young man. He'll marry you.' But Katarina just looked at me. 'And if don't want a baby yet?' she asked. 'I want to see the world, I want . . .' Katarina hammered her fists on the floor. Of course it didn't help any." Grandma sighed and stared at the poor bean plants, as if it was all their fault.

Even from behind my bush, I could see that Mia had the word "abortion" on the tip of her tongue. Fortunately for her, she closed her mouth again—in Grandma's presence a very wise decision.

She, in the meantime, was reporting how she had managed the situation with her rebellious daughter: "'Do you want to ruin your life, child?' I asked her. 'Shake the nonsense out of your head and thank the dear Lord for your Eric. You'll be a good wife to him and a good mother to your child!'—'But what about me? What about me?' Katarina screamed. It was a scream and a sob all at once, and even today I get a chill up my spine when I think about it."

Grandma really did shiver then. "I told her that she wasn't the first and certainly wouldn't be the last to have this happen to her. And that now she had to lie in the bed she'd made for herself, that she had to make the best of it, like all women do."

≈≈≈≈≈

I could hear the blood pounding in my ears. I wished I hadn't heard anything, or that I could forget it all again. Because it was my fault: my mother had been pregnant with *me* and that had ruined all her plans. I had stolen from her the life she had always dreamed of. And one day, she had left us to get it back again.

The two blabbermouths kept right on talking, gossiping about my mother—their voices bored into my head. Dammit, they had no right to spout off about our family like some stupid stars in a trashy tabloid! It just had to stop, no matter what it took!

Swaying, I stood up from my crouched position and came out from behind the blackberries. When the two of them noticed me, they instantly stopped talking. Grandmother's mouth flapped open and shut, which made her look astonishingly similar to our singing plastic fish. In different circumstances, that would have made me laugh.

"Hi," I said quietly.

"Oh, hello, Alexander. I forgot to . . . I need to . . ." She raised her hand and made a vague gesture in the direction of the house, then hobbled off to the patio. No doubt she would pretend the whole episode had never taken place. An excellent idea, in my opinion.

Mia stopped in front of me. The expression on her face was a strange mixture of embarrassment, shame, and pity. I would have liked to shake her.

"I'm sorry," she said.

"What exactly are you sorry about? About what happened, or for sticking your nose into things that are none of your damn business!"

"Both, I guess."

We stared at each other for a while, sizing each other up. "Do you want a drink?" Mia finally asked and held out a battered old tin cup. I took it from her, tipped back a big gulp—and sputtered in surprise. "That's brandy!"

"Your grandmother loves the stuff."

"Aha. Is there anything you don't know about us yet?" I asked, kicking one of the bean stakes angrily with my foot. And almost stepped on a dead eel.

It lay there oddly twisted, like a sign in a secret language. "What the hell is going on here?" I exploded. "What idiotic animal is dragging these fish into our yard?"

Mia raised her eyebrows skeptically. "An animal that gnaws the bones so clean they look like the flesh was burned off by acid? An animal that hangs the rest of the fish in the bushes—like it was marking its territory or something? What kind of an animal would that be?"

What was she talking about?

"No idea," I snarled. "Maybe a cat? Or that dog that's always hanging around here!"

"I've never heard of a dog that catches eels." Mia sighed and nudged the fish with the toe of her shoe. "That's already the third one this week. I find them in between the rosebushes, or in the fruit trees. Fortunately, I can usually throw them in the garbage before your grandmother sees them. She gets upset about it, you know? About the dead fish, the wreaths of mussel shells in the plum trees. Last week I found the torn-off wing of a bird." Mia lowered her voice: "But that's not all. I'm always finding footprints between the rows and the flowerbeds. Haven't you seen them yet, the tracks that go around your house? Someone is watching you, Alex."

"That's absurd!" I snorted. "Who would want to watch us? My family isn't especially interesting." Mia blushed a little. "It has to be some idiots from school," I continued. "Well, I'll teach them a lesson when I catch them! I'll teach them not to pull these stupid stunts on us!"

My rage slowly subsided, leaving me defenseless and exhausted. Thoughts of dead fish and my mother raced through my head. My legs felt weak, and I sank down onto the dusty ground—at a respectable distance from the eel.

With glazed eyes, I stared at the bean stakes, which looked like the bars on a prison window in the harsh sunlight.

How I would have liked to be at the ocean right then! Or anywhere else, far, far away! The main thing was not to be here. Not be me.

Mia stood in front of me and was still looking at me. Her eyes seemed wise, like the eyes of a person who had already experienced a lot. I asked myself what those eyes might have already seen.

"But tell me something about you," I said, tipping back another gulp of brandy. "You seem to be very well informed about the dead fish lying around in our yard. Grandma's already told you all about our family's dirty laundry, but I don't know a thing about you. What's it like where you come from?"

Against her will, Mia crouched down next to me on the ground. She probably only did it for her own conscience. But I didn't let her off the hook. I needed a little distraction.

"So, what's it like in the city?"

"Big," she replied, without batting an eyelash. Apparently, she was playing that game where the first person who blinks, loses. At the moment, I had the feeling I was definitely at a disadvantage. She sat cross-legged next to me, her arms folded tightly over her chest, like a clam inside its shell. Determined not to reveal anything about herself.

But I could play that game, too. "Do you miss it?" I prodded further.

"I miss my cello lessons. I miss browsing in the little stores. But otherwise . . ." Mia shrugged her shoulders. She grabbed the cup with the brandy again. I glanced at her hands as she turned it between her fingers. She had lovely, slim artists' hands, but I noticed that her fingernails were chewed down to the quick.

"What about the people at your old school? Your boyfriend, if you had one?"

"No."

I didn't know if she meant she hadn't had a boyfriend, or that she didn't miss him. But her tone made it clear that she'd tear off my head if I dared continue asking questions.

"And you? I bet you've already had a bunch of girlfriends," she countered.

"But the right one hasn't come along yet," I said, looking her straight in the eyes. Normally girls react to that somehow. They blush, look away quickly, or smile back. Not Mia. No reaction at all, she just shut down. That was a new one for me, a challenge.

"Oh, a romantic," was all she said, and raised her eyebrows mockingly. "I'll bet you're one of those guys who still believes in true love."

When I thought about it, I realized that I actually did. "Yeah, why not?" I said defiantly, because she was acting as if that was something completely ridiculous. "I think there are encounters that can change your life. The right person at the right time. Not forever, but at least for a while. Don't you?"

"Do you really believe that?" Mia's eyes saw through me, and she pressed her lips together. "That whole rose-colored glasses thing is just a bunch of crap. It's all about sex and control."

I stared at her. "If you mean that seriously, then I feel sorry for you."

"You don't have a clue!" Mia jumped up, knocking over the cup. The brandy sank into the dry earth. Her face looked as if something had been spilled, too, and she hissed at me, "Why don't you just get lost and leave me alone?"

I refrained from pointing out that it was my yard I was supposed to vacate. Instead, I bet everything on one card. "Just smile at me one more time, then I'll disappear," I said, looking up at her. "I'll move to Greenland and never, ever come back. And when I'm sitting between the polar bears, your smile will keep me warm."

I could see she was baffled. And I saw the smile sitting at the left corner of her mouth that had just been waiting to show itself. "Well, then get going," Mia answered, "you'd better start packing."

And I had won. Or maybe Mia had won, because although she was laughing now, a hint of sadness remained in her eyes. I sat there and couldn't do anything but look at her.

And suddenly the feeling was there—just like that, no idea where it came from. That feeling I used to get when I stood up on the high dive, bouncing slightly, and then jumped. That sweet pulling in your gut when you fall—fear and happiness at the same time—and you don't want it to stop. Until the water crashes together over your head and you surface again, laughing, breathless.

Chapter 6

Jay

"Shhhh . . ." Alina placed a finger on her lips. There was nothing to hear but our breath, which blended with the wind, and the reeds swaying in the breeze like a woman's hair. I sat completely still, like she had taught me, with my back leaning against the trunk of a silver-tipped willow.

It was our favorite place on the island, shaded by a canopy of slender willow and alder branches woven together. The river rolled along in its bed in front of us, a sluggish, brown-green snake. Sometimes, a ray of sunlight made the water twinkle like a thousand glittering eyes. You should never forget that the river is always hungry.

At the same time, although I couldn't handle it anywhere near as well as Alina, I had tamed it over the years. We had measured our strength against each other while swimming and learned mutual respect. I knew every one of its mud holes for two miles upriver and down, every single rapid, every shallow and deep spot. And it knew mine.

≈≈≈≈≈

Alina nudged me in the side with her elbow again and placed a finger insistently on her lips. *Listen . . . listen very closely . . .* said Alina's eyes, *and learn!*

We were only visitors here. This was no place for humans but the realm of the rampant, thickly entwining plants. A foreign world. "The island doesn't want us," said people in our town, and rumor had it that this place was haunted.

But the island seemed to accept us. Alina had even given it a new name; she called it the Island of Bliss. And what Alina said was the rule.

So I tried it, I tried really hard. To listen. I heard the birds in the thicket, how they quarreled only to turn around and announce their reconciliation even louder. Occasionally, you could hear the slap of a wing or a splash as a fish sank back into the streaming calmness of the river. That was all.

What was the point? I wrinkled my forehead in a scowl. This game was getting boring, and one of my legs was already starting to fall asleep.

The corners of Alina's mouth curled into a mocking smile, and she smoothed the folds in my forehead with a finger. *You think too much!* Her left sleeve dripped. Her eyes were green-brown, like the river.

Then she took my hand. And just like that, as if someone had turned the dial on a stereo receiver, the sounds suddenly seemed clearer. At the same time, my thoughts fled like sand. All at once, I was wide awake, fully present.

Together, we fell back into the damp spring grass. High above us were the clouds in blue, the thin membrane of the sky that arched with our every breath.

How long we lay there like that, I couldn't have said later. I only remember the dragonflies that landed in Alina's hair like glittering jewelry. I remember the disbelieving, astonishing joy it brought to simply lie there, breathing in sync with her. To look at her.

No words. Just the humming of insects, an underlying, vibrating pulse. I felt it deep within me; it combined with my heartbeat. And then, in that moment, I heard it.

My heart beat in the old willow tree I had been leaning against, pounded in the snail that glided across my arm in slow motion, leaving behind a silver trail. I was in the snail, in the blades of grass that cast feathery shadows on our bodies. Everywhere. I became immortal.

I sank into the earth; the grass immediately sprouted through my fingers. The sound of growing grass surrounded us, the clicking and humming of the tiny creatures that inhabited it. No words.

Just us, facing each other, as the new green growth shot up all around us with a rustle. Alina's smile.

First Intermezzo

How long can a person survive in ice-cold water?

Not very long, *whispers a voice in my head. It seems like I've already been stuck in this hole in the ice for hours. As if my "not very long" will soon be at an end.*

But I don't want to die yet!

Pull yourself together, I order myself. Stay calm, very calm, otherwise you're as good as dead! Try to hoist yourself up on the ice . . . that's right, farther, a little bit more . . .

It doesn't work! I just don't have any more strength. Gradually, it's becoming clear to me that I'll never make it out of here on my own.

What an idiot! Why didn't I think of it earlier! Any normal person in my situation would scream for help. Someone will hear me, then they'll come and finally get me out of here. Save me!

Adrenaline shoots through my body, hot and vital. I open my mouth. . . . I've never screamed for help in my entire life, but now I'm going to do it. Now I have to do it.

"Help!"

I'm going to be at home, lying in my warm, cozy bed . . .

"Help, I fell through the ice!"

. . . and drink hot chocolate. With a hot water bottle at my feet. Soon, soon . . .

No one comes. Why doesn't anyone come, where are those idiots? Are they all deaf, dammit? They're sitting inside all warm in front of the television while I'm out here dying a miserable death!

"Please, help me someone, help!" I implore the air, the bare willows, the sky. "Why won't anyone help me?" My voice cracks. I'm hoarse, but I continue yelling. If I'm screaming, I'm not dead! I scream until I can only manage a croak, until there's nothing left inside me except emptiness.

I try to fill it with something warm. Exhausted, I close my eyes and imagine lying on the pleasantly warm wooden dock on a summer's day. The sun paints circles on my stomach. My tongue tastes of cherries . . .

And for a split second, I'm almost there. Warm and happy.

But then the moldy, stale smell of the stagnant winter river fills my nose. The feeling turns to dust and disintegrates in the air and cold.

What remains is only the cutting certainty: no one will come to save me. We broke our blood oath. This is the punishment. I'm on my own now.

My face is wet; I think I'm crying.

"Help me," I whisper, but the sluggish gurgling of the river drowns out my words.

Desperately, I try to bring summer back into my head.

L'ESTATE
SUMMER

Chapter 7

Mia

Today I was in good form: I made the bow dance over the strings, made the cello purr, and sing, and cry.

At first, you feel your way from note to note, stumbling, trying hard to do everything exactly right. Like a hiker laboriously making her way up a steep mountain path, you slave away at it . . . and then suddenly you're at the peak. There you are, and there is the music. And in that moment you belong together. You look down at the landscape of sound spread out below you and recognize that it's your own personal landscape, the one inside of you.

Only then, when your hands just do what they need to, when you reach that dream-like state where everything else blurs and becomes meaningless. When the bow is practically an extension of your hand and you don't know anymore where your instrument ends and you begin, then you're really making music.

Every movement is the only right one at exactly the right moment. My body dissolved. I wished I could play into eternity. Then life would be tolerable.

~~~~~

When the piece came to an end and I lowered my bow, I still felt slightly dazed. To clear my head, I stepped over to the open window and drew deep breaths of the air that smelled of summer. I admired the leaves of my cherry tree, moving like green silk in the June breeze.

The tree stared back at me.

I blinked. But there was no doubt—through the tangle of branches, two eyes glittered back at me!

"Aaaaaaaaaahhh!" I yelled, stumbling away from the window.

The thing in the tree screamed, too. Then I heard breaking and splintering as it fell through the tree branches toward the ground. "Ooww!" It sounded bad.

Holding my cello bow in front of me like a dagger, I crept back to the window and peered outside. Under the cherry tree, in a hail of leaves and unripe cherries torn from the tree, lay Jay! He flailed his arms and legs like a beetle that's fallen on its back.

"What . . . what on earth are you doing in my tree, you . . . you pervert!" I screeched as soon as I had recovered enough from my shock to make a sound at all. My voice cracked, and I could tell I was close to becoming hysterical. I was shaking all over.

With a pitiful groan, Jay sat up and rubbed his back. "I'm not a . . . I didn't mean to . . ." he stammered as blood flushed his cheeks red with indignation.

"What were you DOING there, then, dammit?" At the moment, I had a strong urge to impale him with my bow.

"Listening!" Jay blurted out. "I was just listening!"

For a moment, we were both silent in our exhaustion. Slowly, I calmed down enough that I could look at the situation more objectively. I studied Jay, all scratched up, suspiciously—and had to admit that he didn't exactly look like a lurking rapist. Crazy but harmless.

I took a deep breath. "Maybe it would be better if you come up here so we can talk about this face-to-face."

I went downstairs to open the door for him, and Jay limped right behind me on the way back up to my room. His eyes swept the room with curiosity and stopped as soon as he saw my cello. He literally couldn't take his eyes off it.

"Do you like classical music?" I asked when the silence finally started to become too awkward for me.

"I guess so," Jay mumbled, without taking his eyes off the instrument. Good heavens, had the guy never seen a cello before? "But I don't know much classical music. My grandma always listens to easy-listening music."

Apparently, the poor thing was growing up in a cultural wasteland!

"Is that it?" Jay asked eagerly, "Your singing heart?"

"Uh . . . that's my cello, if that's what you mean," I replied, bewildered. Jay was a strange guy.

His eyes asked me for permission before he touched it. Shyly, almost reverently, he stroked the instrument as if it were a living creature.

I wanted to see what would happen—so I plucked one of the strings. I could see how the sound moved through his hand pressed flat against the wood, through his arm, and lit up his face.

"I feel it right in here," Jay whispered, placing a hand on his heart. His face registered a fervent wonder that until that moment I had only seen in young children. As if he had never learned to pretend or put on an act, to bury his feelings behind masks.

Then Jay even laid his face on the glistening wood to feel the vibrations of the note as it faded away—without any shyness about acting like an idiot in front of me. Gaping in surprise, I stared at him as if he were a strange, exotic animal, fascinated by his apparent lack of self-consciousness as he followed his sudden impulses.

"Please," Jay said, looking at me as if I were a magician able to weave music with her bare hands, "please play something else!"

I couldn't help myself. I felt flattered. Even more, I felt electrified, swept up in his childish enthusiasm. "Okay, let's see if you like this." I put a CD in my CD player and settled into playing position. After hectically fumbling around and then finding the right notes, I pressed the play button on the remote control.

My room had excellent acoustics. The notes dripped, surged, and bubbled from the bare walls. Jay stood in the middle of the room surrounded by the cascade of sounds.

His eyes were closed, his arms slightly raised with the palms turned upward. It wouldn't have surprised me if he had suddenly stuck out his tongue to catch the sounds like snowflakes, to taste them.

If someone else had done that, it would have seemed fake and absurd but not with Jay. It touched me deeply. I had never seen someone listen to music so intensely, practically bathing in it with his entire body. In fact, I had never met anyone like Jay.

Only when the last bars of the piece had faded away did he open his eyes again. He said just one word: "Summer."

"You do know it, then," I said, a little disappointed. "You're right, it was "Summer" from Vivaldi's *Four Seasons*."

Jay smiled and shook his head. "I swear, I'd never heard of it before. But it sounded like when you're sitting in a tree in June while the wind rustles in the leaves . . . just like . . . like eating cherries!"

"Really?" I replied skeptically. Jay nodded his confirmation. "Do you play an instrument, too?" I asked curiously. "You seem to have a good feel for music."

"I don't know. Sometimes we sing out there on the island, Alina and I. But not with music," he added quickly. "Just spontaneously, for us. For the river and the grass and the kingfishers."

"Who is Alina?"

"Alina and I . . . we . . ." Jay broke off and tried to put his words together again. Thoughtfully, like someone trying to build a tall tower out of building blocks, he continued. "She taught me to sing. How to imitate the call of a kingfisher. And of course how to swim. . . . One day she just threw me into the river, and that's how I learned. Alina taught me all of that, all kinds of things that are important!"

Jay's eye, the green-brown one, gleamed. He leaned over toward me, as if to share a secret with me. "She's my best friend . . . she is . . . she's everything to me!" he whispered. "Alina is my whole world. And I'm hers."

I didn't know how to react to this declaration. "That . . . that must be nice," I replied lamely.

Jay nodded soberly. "But it's different from your music. May I . . . may I come again and listen?"

"You're welcome to but I'd prefer if you told me beforehand. Maybe knock on the window or something so I know you're there. And we also have a front door with a doorbell." I was gratified to see that he blushed. "And I have another request," I added. "Sometime I'd like to come and hear you singing. That's only fair, right?"

Jay chewed on his lower lip awkwardly and thought about it. "Good," he finally answered after a long pause, "it's a deal!"

He insisted on shaking my hand.

I watched him as he trotted home with a stack of my best classical music CDs, which I had loaned him. *Encounters of the third kind*, I thought, and for some reason I had to laugh.

≈ ≈ ≈ ≈ ≈

The next day, I had no reason to laugh. That was the day I found the dead pike in my room.

It had probably been dead for a few days already, at least judging from the smell. Its long body had been torn open

77

and the guts were strewn across my floor. The fish's mouth with its pointy teeth seemed to be twisted into an evil grin.

I ran down the stairs to get my mother. She was as horrified as I was.

"Peeew, is that a stench!" she groaned and pulled the tail of her shirt over her face as she stared at the remains of the fish in disgust. There was concern in her voice as she asked, "Are you having trouble with the kids at your new school, sweetheart? Is there anyone you think might do something horrendous like this?"

I shrugged my shoulders. "I don't have any enemies, if that's what you mean." That sentence sounded like something that had wandered out of a mobster movie and into our lives. It scared us both.

"Someone probably threw the fish through the open window," my mother murmured. "Don't worry about it, Mia. I'm sure it's nothing but a stupid stunt pulled by some country bumpkins." It was clear to me that she didn't quite believe what she was saying.

I didn't, either.

The dead fish was a warning, I was sure of that. And I also knew exactly where the warning came from. But what had I done to draw the attention of the shadow that was lurking around the Stonebrooks' house?

"It really *has* to be a prank, doesn't it?" My mother studied me carefully.

For a moment, I considered telling her about the fish cadavers in the neighbors' yard, and the footprints between the rows of vegetables in their garden. But the Stonebrooks apparently hadn't thought it necessary to inform the police yet. What good would that have done? At most, they could have filed a complaint against unknown persons. After all, there was no evidence. Nothing but a few dead fish.

I nodded weakly. "Yeah, Mom. It's definitely just a dumb prank."

≈ ≈ ≈ ≈ ≈

It took me hours to clean my room. The stench of decay hung stubbornly between the walls, clung to the clothes in my closet.

But that wasn't all. It was little things. My hairbrush lay in a different place. Some of my CDs were scratched and only played shrill, dissonant melodies that hurt my ears.

Two of the strings on my cello were broken. I held my instrument in my arms for a long time and stroked the smooth, red-brown wood to soothe my nerves.

Nothing truly terrible had happened. The strings were easily replaced. Maybe I was slowly getting paranoid? It could just be a series of coincidences.

But deep inside I knew that someone had secretly been in my room. I could feel it. A presence was like a blight that defiled everything. My white walls were contaminated, as if they had become murky. The shadows from the branches of the cherry tree flitting across them seemed threatening now.

I looked outside at my tree. For a good climber, it wouldn't be difficult to get into my room by clambering across its wide branches. But if there had ever been wet footprints on the stone path in our yard, the sun had long since made them disappear.

I didn't say anything to my parents to keep from worrying them even more. But from that day on, I always kept my window shut when I wasn't in my room.

While the cherries slowly ripened on the other side of the glass panes, I tried to forget the whole thing. It worked pretty well, and that was mainly thanks to Alex.

Chapter 8

Alexander

⅏⅏

The smell of freshly mown grass and ozone filled the air, and the riverbanks were pink with blossoming spring herbs. In the June sunshine, I strolled past Mia's house on my way to meet up with the guys at the bridge. Suddenly, a cherry pit skittered across the dusty path in front of me.

"Hey, Alex!" a voice called.

I looked up and saw Mia sitting in the crown of the tree. If my grandmother had been sitting on that thick branch, I could hardly have been more astonished.

"What are you doing up there?" What an idiotic question! Cherries dangled from her ears, juice ran down her chin. She looked downright cheerful! That's a word I would never have expected to associate with her.

"I'm following a friend's suggestion," Mia replied, peering down at me. "Eating cherries is supposed to feel like music."

"And?"

She plucked a dark red cherry from its stem with her lips, closed her eyes, and chewed thoughtfully. "Mmm . . . yeesss."

"Will you throw one down for me?" I called, opening my mouth wide. From among the leaves came a sound that sounded awfully close to a giggle. Then a cherry landed on the path, three steps in front of me. Somewhat bruised, but still perfectly edible. I popped it into my mouth. "You missed—amateur!"

The second one hit my shoulder, the third even landed on my nose. Mia was a quick study. "Not bad. But wouldn't you rather come down from there? Then you might even get one in!"

"Nah. Not really," Mia grinned. The sun shone through the leaves and glistened on her hair. The coloring was slowly growing out, and you could see that her natural color was a warm chestnut.

The sight of Mia perched up there reminded me of a children's riddle that Grandma annoyed us with every summer: "A young girl sits in a tree wearing a red skirt. In her heart is a stone. Now what can that be?"

"That's easy! A cherry!" Mia laughed.

"Wrong, it's *you*!" I teased her. "With a stone heart that won't soften enough for you to come down and share your cherries with me! Alright then, I'll climb up to you."

I started climbing up the tree, which wasn't so hard. The smooth bark felt like warm skin under my fingers. While I swung from branch to branch, a bombardment of cherries rained down on me. The fruits burst on my body and left blotches on my T-shirt and bare arms. Small, blood red marks. Like tiny wounds.

And then, finally, I reached her branch. I think we were both surprised by the sudden intimacy. Our faces were almost touching; out of breath, we stared at each other.

I studied her face: the pale, delicate skin; the narrow nose; her dark brown eyes with the long lashes. Her softly curving lips. From her earlobes dangled her shell earrings. My heart was pounding in my chest. "You have thousands of freckles," I finally said.

That was the wrong thing to say! Mia's face, still warm from the exertion of throwing, began to set in its old, familiar, closed expression. Like water freezing over. It made me cold to see it happening.

"If you can't get one in now, you're totally blind," I said quickly to counter it, squeezing my eyes shut and opening my mouth as absurdly wide as a wide-mouthed frog.

Then I felt Mia very gently place a cherry on my tongue. The full sweetness exploded in my mouth.

The ground was no longer firm. The wind rustled in the leaves of the cherry tree. Everything around us was in swaying motion, as if the two of us were alone on a green ship. *Like somewhere on the high seas*, I thought. *It must feel exactly like this.*

Shadows of leaves trembled on her face. Oh, God, I wanted to kiss her.

And then, I had no idea how it came about, but I did it. I kissed Mia!

Immediately, I felt her body stiffen.

Oh, no, I had misread the signs! *You blew it, Alex, you idiot!*

I wanted to pull back from her and frantically wracked my pathetic brain for apologies, when I noticed it. Her tongue tentatively nudged me, made the acquaintance of mine. She tasted like cherries, a little bit like chocolate, and buried underneath that, very faintly, of Mia.

I always closed my eyes when I was kissing. But when I opened them again, I noticed that she was observing me with a fixed gaze, sizing me up, somehow.

"My heart isn't a stone," she said in a serious tone.

"No," I whispered, confused by the odd expression on her face. Only much later would I realize that her words had been a warning.

Mia exhaled deeply and relaxed. Her breath caressed my skin warmly like a fleeting touch. Yes, it felt like music. It felt like summer.

"Kiss me again, Alex," she whispered.

Chapter 9

Jay

||||||||||||||||||||||||||||||||||||||||||||||||||||||||||||||||||||||||||||||||||||||||||||||||||||||||||||||||||||||||||||||||||||||||||

The bedsheets Grandma had attached to the clothesline with clothespins fluttered in the wind like white clouds. I captured their crackling on my voice recorder before they could fly away into the summer skies again.

But there was some kind of annoying muttering in the background. I peered past the sheets toward the river, where Grandma and Papa had nothing better to do than ruin my recording.

"And what do you want to do now, Eric?" Grandma's voice bored into my father's back as he sat on the dock and played hide-and-seek with the old pike.

"About what?" Papa grumbled back. But I heard in his voice that he knew exactly what she was talking about.

Grandma put her hands on her hips. "About the pictures, of course! We talked about it already last year, that it can't go on this way. . . . Alexander is almost grown up now!"

She slammed him into the ground with her words. I saw how Papa shrank into himself on his camping stool. He probably would have been glad to trade places with Old George, the pike, right then.

"But Alex is always so happy. Those pictures are important to him!" he protested.

"It was a mistake from the very beginning to agree to this whole thing. I thought it would make it easier for the boys. But instead, everything has just gotten more complicated." Grandma muttered something like, "When something like that gets to be a habit. . . . I told you right off: a lie is a lie and can only bring unhappiness."

"All right, I'll call her and explain it to her," Papa finally said with a sigh. "There won't be any more photos coming."

I didn't completely understand what they were talking about, but I knew one thing for sure: it would be a sad birthday for my brother.

Papa's line jerked, and he quickly started to reel it in. He clearly thought the conversation was over.

It was just as obvious that Grandma didn't think so. "Good, then that's settled," she said, but made no move to leave.

My father grimly worked his fishing rod. Hanging from the bait at the end of the line flapped not Old George, but a small silvery fish.

"Damn, too small," Papa grumbled, in a foul mood.

"Will you talk to the boys, too?" Grandma continued the topic. "They're both old enough for the truth. Sometimes I'm not sure how much they still remember. Not so much Alexander, but Jay. He's never asked about her, not a single time. As if he . . ." A sad laugh rattled in her throat, like the boiler of an old steam engine. "He was so young then."

My father didn't answer. Carefully, very gently, he released the fish from the hook and threw it back into the river.

But I knew as well as he did that it wouldn't help. That's how it is with the fish. They swallow the hook because they see what they want to see. When you try to free them from it to put them back in the water, they die anyway. Papa always said they never recovered from the injury. Something in their mouths is damaged so badly that they can't eat anymore. That's why they die.

But I think they die of disappointment over this world riddled with hooks.

Grandma hobbled back up to the house, past the clothesline, without noticing me. But my father sat out there for a while longer. He looked at the fish blood on his hands, glistening in the sun.

~~~~~

The bedsheets didn't sing for me again that day. At some point, I gave up and wandered a ways upriver. There, I crouched in the grass at the riverbank.

I felt so strange. My belly hurt as if I had a millstone in my stomach. Miserable, I stared into the water flowing by.

"What should I do?" I asked my reflection, which trembled in the current like a candle's flame. Should I tell Skip what I had just heard? Strange, until now I had never had to ask myself this question. Skip took care of Skip. And Skip took care of Jay.

Could it work the other way around, too?

My face hovered before me in the water, a blurry oval with two different-colored eyes.

Monster eyes, Wolf and Matt used to call me when Skip couldn't hear them. Suddenly, I had a strong urge to throw a rock at my reflection to see how it broke apart.

I quickly searched for a stone, drew back . . . and my eyes became her eyes. Her features replaced mine as she slowly surfaced.

I lowered my fist clutching the stone. Alina stood before me in chest-deep water.

"Where did you come from?" I asked, astonished.

"You called me, didn't you?" Alina turned onto her back in the water, as agile and quick as an otter, and sprayed me in the face with a splash of water.

In a way, I had. "Yeah, well, I have a problem and could use your advice. It's about Skip," I stalled, not sure how I should start. "His birthday is coming up and . . ."

Alina made a face as if she had a toothache. "I don't help pick out birthday presents if I'm not even invited to the party! Skip doesn't want to see me, you know that."

"But it's not even about a stupid birthday present, it's something much more important!" I protested indignantly. "Let me finish explaining!"

Alina pouted. "Oh, stop talking and get in the water already, Jay. What do we care about other people's problems? The only important thing is you and me."

I didn't say a word.

"Let's go for a swim, Jay." Alina drew her fingers through the water and smiled at me.

I felt myself nodding. I had just enough time to peel the clothes off my body before Alina grabbed my arm and pulled me into the river with her.

Chapter 10

Mia

||||||||||||||||||||||||||||||||||||||||||||||||||||||||||||||||||||||||||||||||||||||||||||||||||||||||||||

Alex wasn't at home.

"He's still behind the counter at the snack bar," his grandmother called to me from the porch. "But if you can make do with Jay and I for a change, you can come join us for a piece of cake." There was a hint of an accusation in her tone. I immediately felt a twinge of guilt. I had pretty much given up our chats recently.

"I'd be happy to join you!" I quickly responded.

A few minutes later, I sat next to Jay at the dining room table as his grandmother piled enormous pieces of redcurrant tart on our plates. I was thinking that she had never continued her story and told me what happened to Katarina next. But there wasn't any room in my head for other people's stories right now, anyway.

There was only room for Alex and me.

I still didn't know exactly how I had slipped into this "relationship," but we'd been together for about a month now. Alex made me laugh, and I had been laughing a lot the past few weeks. It had been months since I had felt so lighthearted, even happy, and I wanted to enjoy it while it lasted. I had forbidden myself to brood about where this thing inevitably had to lead.

The currant cream melted on my tongue like a wonderful, fleeting dream. "Mmmm!" Jay agreed, starting to help himself to a second piece.

"Nothing doing, young man!" his grandmother protested, slapping his fingers. "That's Alexander's birthday cake! He should at least get a decent piece of that, since there won't be any mail for him." She moved a hand across her face, as if to wipe away the words she had started to say. Then she abruptly began clearing the table.

Jay walked me to the door. "You won't forget Skip's party tonight, will you?"

I rolled my eyes. "How could I forget his birthday? Alex has been talking about it nonstop for days! I've never met anyone who was so excited about his birthday."

Jay sighed quietly. "That's because ... well, Skip's parties are always the big event of the year here," he continued with a crooked grin. "After all, he has the keys to the swimming pool!"

It seemed to me that he had wanted to say something else.

~~~~~

Of course, I had been to other parties in the city, even snuck into a nightclub. But nothing had prepared me for what would happen that night.

91

It was one of those summer nights when people toss and turn in their damp sheets, too restless to sleep. The heat of the July day still clung heavily to everything. I could feel it radiating from the pavement through the soles of my sandals as I walked along the path to the pool. Even the leaves on the trees seemed to reflect the sun's burning rays, and even though it was almost ten o'clock at night, it was astonishingly bright out.

As I drew closer to the park, I could hear high-spirited voices and booming music, like the beating of an enormous heart.

The gatehouse was deserted, and the gates to the swimming pool stood wide open. Behind them, shadowy figures moved around in the twilight. It looked like half the teenagers in town were gathered here, especially judging by the number of inflatable mats floating around the black surface of the water. I even spotted the plastic outline of a Caribbean island, complete with palm trees!

On the cement slabs, a big bonfire burned. I moved toward the group standing around it. Some people were dancing to the music. The flames threw flickering light on their bare skin, since most of the guests were only wearing bathing suits. In my black top and gypsy skirt, I felt like a crane surrounded by beautiful birds of paradise.

Laughter surrounded me, and the crackle of sparks flew skyward like tiny orange fireflies. Faces appeared in the circle of light from the fire and then faded back into the night, but none of them belonged to Alex.

I did see his brother, though. His head tilted to the side, a fist pressed against his ear, Jay was crouched on the opposite side of the fire. Finally, someone I could talk to.

"Hey, Jay!" I called, making my way toward him. "What are you doing there?"

Slowly, Jay uncurled his fist—and showed me a tiny voice recorder in the palm of his hand. "I'm recording my own Four Seasons," he explained in a serious tone.

"Uh huh," I replied, only slightly interested. "Where's your brother? I haven't even said happy birthday yet."

Jay closed his eyes briefly and listened, then pointed, without looking, in the distance. "Over there!"

Sure enough, there he stood with his friend Wolf and a couple other guys. The whole group didn't give the impression of being especially sober anymore.

"Happy birthday, Alex!" I gave him a hug, even though it felt kind of weird to me in front of his staring friends. "Here's your present," I said awkwardly, handing him my package.

"Ooooh," Wolf said with a leer. "Come on guys, I think we're in the way here." With whistles and jeers, they went away.

"I hope you like it," I said as Alex unwrapped his present.

After much deliberation, I had finally decided on a little travel atlas because Alex had once told me that his greatest desire was to move away from this hick town. "I want to travel and see the world, you know, Mia? The ocean!"

As he tore open the wrapping paper, I was already anticipating the excitement I had seen in his eyes then. But no, there wasn't even a hint of it! Alex just leafed through the pages covered with pictures of exotic places and muttered, "Cool, thanks."

I was disappointed, maybe even a little insulted. Alex didn't even notice. He looked right past me, as if he didn't know I was there. "Is . . . are you okay?" I asked hesitantly, staring at him.

"Yeah, sure. Everything's great!" he answered, but his eyes flickered as he spoke. "And you, are you having a good time?"

"Mmmm."

"Me, too. Do you want a beer?" Without waiting for an answer, he tried to casually open a beer bottle. "Damn!" The bottle opener had slipped and cut his hand. Alex sucked on the bleeding wound, then spit it out and laughed.

Usually, I got a warm feeling in my stomach when he laughed, but now I wished he would stop it. It was giving me goose bumps.

"That works, too," Alex laughed, and let a few drops of blood fall into his bottle of beer. "Now we can drink a blood oath! Hey, Jay, remember how we used to do that?" he called over to his younger brother.

"Sure!" Jay came trotting over to us. For the second time that evening, I was glad to see him.

"What kind of ancient macho ritual is that?" I joked, trying to hide my insecurity. "You two must have watched too many Western movies when you were little!"

"This isn't a stupid kid's game!" Alex snapped at me unexpectedly. "It means that you're there for each other— that you can really count on each other!"

"Exactly!" Jay echoed. He explained, looking professional, "Blood brothers stick together forever. Nothing in the world can come between them! They don't have any secrets from each other."

No secrets. I had to think of Nicolas then, and that I had absolutely no intention of telling Alex anything about him or that whole sorry episode.

I swallowed. "And if you can't keep this blood oath?" I protested. Both brothers stared at me. "I just mean those are really high standards, aren't they?" I squeaked in a small voice.

"Anyone who breaks the oath is a traitor," Alex replied coldly. But it was Jay's words that scared me more: "If you broke the oath, it would make everyone very unhappy," he said quietly and sadly. "Then each of us would be all alone."

I had a safety pin on my skirt. Ceremoniously, Jay and I pricked our fingers with it and let a few drops of blood fall into the bottle of beer. Then the bottle was passed around.

Each of the three of us took a swig. I threw mine back so fast that I almost choked on it—yuck, was that revolting!

"Do you feel it? Now we're bound together for ever and ever!" Alex said. His face glowed in the firelight. I didn't feel anything. Instead, I asked myself in what kind of a freakish place I had landed here.

~~~~~

Suddenly, we heard a loud splash. The people who had been standing around the bonfire streamed over to the pool as if something were being given away for free.

"I don't believe it, they're actually starting without me! Wait for me, you idiots!" Alex yelled, and off he went.

I turned to Jay. "Can you please explain to me what's going on with your brother?" For the first time since I'd known him, Jay seemed sad.

"It's because Skip always gets a package on his birthday. Photos from his mother."

His choice of words was odd; after all, Katarina was *his* mother, too.

"But today he didn't get any pictures," Jay concluded with a sigh, as if he had just explained everything. He gestured toward the party, the fire slowly burning down. "All of this is just ashes in the wind for Skip, nothing but ashes."

I was still thinking about this comment as we quickly moved toward the swimming pool, too. Lots of kids were already sitting on the edge of the pool, dangling their legs in the water and eagerly staring up at the diving tower. "Come on, get on with it, you cowards!" someone yelled.

That's when I first noticed the divers up on the high dive. Their silhouettes were only vague against the backdrop of the star-studded night sky. Animated by the cheers and whistles of the crowd, they took a running start and plunged from the tower into the void. They smacked the surface of the water in such quick succession that their bodies seemed to almost touch each other in the air.

Impressive fountains of spray spouted up. The water drops sparkled in the moonlight, soaked the hem of my skirt, and covered the faces of the screaming spectators.

"Splaaaassshh!" cried Jay, who was standing next to me. He drew out the letters in such a unique way that it sounded astonishingly like an actual spray of water.

"So why aren't you up there with them? Don't you want to prove how brave and manly you are?" I asked in a teasing way.

But Jay just looked at me uncomprehendingly. "I don't like it. You could fall up there . . . fall out of the world."

His words got lost in the hoots and jeers of the crowd because the divers' tricks were getting harder and riskier. Wolf did a somersault and Matt surfaced after a cannonball, coughing and spitting out water.

And then came Alex.

Swaying slightly he stepped onto the diving board and bowed, like the ringmaster at a circus, to his audience. Suddenly, everything grew quiet; only the water gurgled as it slapped against the edge of the pool. I didn't want to believe my eyes when I saw what came next: Alex did a handstand up there at the end of the diving board—ten feet up in the air!

He could break his neck! *Have you completely lost your mind!* I wanted to yell at him, but it was too late.

Slowly, almost in slow motion, Alex let himself tip over toward the water.

My heart pounded in fear like a broken lawn mower. Instinctively, I closed my eyes, and only opened them again when everyone around me broke into wild applause.

Then I saw Alex, all in one piece, climbing out of the pool. He disappeared into the darkness, and the crowd of spectators gradually broke up, too.

"Wow, that was the best jump Alex has ever done!" Jay said, next to me, deeply impressed.

"That was a completely idiotic, suicidal show!" I said through gritted teeth. My heartbeat had slowed down by then, but anger and concern remained. "Come on, Jay, help me look for this crazy nut before he accidently kills himself with one of his stunts!"

≈≈≈≈≈

We finally found Alex at the top of the diving platform, where he lay stretched out flat on the diving board. He stared dully into the water, where a shaky moon was reflected, almost full and so blindingly white it looked like someone had cut a piece out of the black night sky with a sharp blade.

I stayed close to the exit and held tight to the railing. Just looking around was making me dizzy.

"What are you doing up here?" I said cautiously, not wanting to scare him.

"I'm trying to remember," Alex replied, then took a swig from his beer.

"What?"

But he didn't answer.

≈≈≈≈≈

Somehow, I finally managed to convince Alex that he'd be a whole lot more comfortable in his bed than up there on the diving platform. Together with Jay, I steered him toward home.

"You're my angel, Mia," Alex mumbled as I helped him to his feet when he stumbled. In gratitude, he tried to plant a big kiss on my cheek. He stank of alcohol. Disgusted, I turned my head. Jay giggled.

I came within an inch of leaving the two brothers stranded in the middle of nowhere—the two of them could figure out how to make their way home without me. But just an hour earlier I had drunk their blood, and I felt obligated, somehow.

That, however, was before Alex started singing sentimental songs about lonesome sailors. I was starting to understand how he had come by the nickname Skip! On top of everything, Jay joined in with a rousing "What should we do with a drunken sailor!"

"Ssshhhhhh," I warned as we navigated the narrow steps inside their house. "Or do you want to wake up your grandmother?"

That got their attention. Jay disappeared into his room, and I thought what a relief it would be to slip away and go home.

But instead, Alex grabbed my hand and pulled me into his dark room. "Wait—I want to show you something."

Carefully, as if it could disintegrate into dust any moment, he placed something cool and smooth in the palm of my hand. It was a large shell. The mother-of-pearl lining the inside caught the moonlight, and it glistened like a hidden treasure.

I had a sneaking suspicion that he was sharing something very special with me. "Hold it up to your ear!" Alex whispered. I did.

Caught in the spirals of the shell was the echo of a sound. "Do you hear that?" Alex asked excitedly. I nodded, and the happiest smile slowly spread across his face. And then, I recognized that in spite of all their differences, they were similar after all, he and Jay. Although I had always found Alex much more practical and down to earth than his younger brother, he had the same enchanted smile, not quite of this world.

Waves crashing on a faraway beach ...

"That's the ocean, Mia!"

And I almost believed it! I shook myself to shake off the illusion. "That isn't the ocean. It's the sound of your own blood in your ears, Alex!"

"You mean the ocean is inside me?" His smile became a notch dimmer, slipped.

I suddenly felt mean, as if I had stolen something from him, destroyed something on purpose.

Alex took the shell from my hand. "Nonsense!" he declared in a surly tone, and fell backward on his bed. "Of course it's the ocean!"

I didn't contradict him anymore. If he really wanted to believe that, he could go right ahead! What right did I have to interfere? Feeling uncomfortable, I chewed on my fingernails. Suddenly, I wanted to get out of this room, where the sloped walls were plastered with layers and layers of photographs, like the walls of a shrine.

Alex had changed the décor since I had last been here. Instead of all the pictures of South America with their warm jungle colors, the walls were covered with photos of Greenland: icebergs shimmering glacier blue and cold. Endless vistas of snow.

I shivered. All at once, I could feel Alex observing me with bloodshot eyes.

"She just left us," he said suddenly, without any transition. "Without a word, without an explanation."

It was hard to follow his train of thought, but then I understood that he was talking about his mother. He had never told me anything about her, and I had never had the courage to ask him about her. "We don't mean anything to her. Not Jay, not me. And now she's forgotten us entirely."

"How would you know that?" I contradicted, but the words sounded forced even to me.

"No one leaves people they love. Not like that."

There was no arguing with the bare truth of that. I didn't say anything. Lying on the bed, Alex looked up at me. "You're going to leave me, too," he said calmly. There was no accusation in his voice, nothing other than this bare statement. "I saw it in your eyes, they gave you away. You always run away from me."

"What are you saying?" I stuttered. "That's . . . that's not true. I . . ." But deep, deep inside me, in that protected place no one was allowed to see, I knew that Alex was right.

I felt like I had been caught red-handed. Exposed. My throat burned with shame, or maybe it was tears, I don't know. I swallowed the burn as I helplessly searched for comforting words.

"But think of our oath!" I whispered, because nothing else occurred to me. "We took a blood oath . . . that each of us will always be there for the others. I won't leave you. Do you hear me? I'm not going to leave you."

I lay down next to Alex on the bed and held his hand, whispering these words over and over again like a mantra meant to soothe both of us. I kept it up until I heard his breathing becoming deeper and steady and only got up when I was sure he had fallen asleep. Carefully, I tried to free my hand from his grip, but his fingers were clutching mine so tightly I had to pry them open one at a time.

In his sleep, Alex looked younger. The sight of his hand lying on the pillow empty and relaxed led to a sudden pang of sadness.

With his other hand, he still held the shell to his ear, as if he were listening to something.

Chapter 11

Alexander

"I'll never touch alcohol again!" I vowed when I woke up the morning after the party with a wicked hangover. My head pounded as if a sadistic elf with a jackhammer were boring through my brain.

While I fumbled around in the drawer of my nightstand for an aspirin, the memory of what had transpired the night before began to surface. *No letter, no letter, no letter . . .*

I had tried to drink myself unconscious at my party. Apparently, it hadn't worked, because a few cells of gray matter were still working. Unfortunately, I still had fragmented memories of what had happened the previous night. Mia had brought me home—tucked me into bed, to be more precise, while I talked endlessly about some embarrassing nonsense. With a groan, I fell back onto the pillows. Spend the night with Alex Stonebrook and you can really experience something, ha ha!

My gaze landed on the travel atlas that Mia had given me, lying on the desk. Idiot that I am, I hadn't even properly thanked her for it. I groaned even louder.

But I would make it up to her. I swore it. I even had an idea how I could do it.

~~~~~

Although it was late, there were still lights on at the Reinholds' house. But not in Mia's room. Had she forgotten that we had a date?

Only after I had thrown the third handful of gravel against the glass did she finally open her window. "Cut that out, Alex! I'm coming already!" she hissed down to me. I grinned and blended in with the nighttime shadows of the cherry tree again.

Suddenly, I stopped short. Something was dangling from one of the upper branches. It was hanging right in front of Mia's window, but I could only vaguely see its outline. Curious, I climbed up the tree until I reached it.

It was a doll, a small doll made of faded rags. It was hanging by a string that was wound around its neck like a noose. I carefully freed it.

Once I had reached firm ground again, I examined my find more closely. The eyes were pieces of shell, and the rest of the face was roughly drawn with charcoal. But I recognized immediately who the doll was supposed to represent by the clump of reddish-brown hair that someone had attached to its head.

Then I had to think of the story about the dead pike that Mia had told me a while ago. *"That stench everywhere! My whole room was infested with it, Alex. It might sound silly, but I knew someone had been in there, and had been touching my things. My cello, the CDs, even my hairbrush."*

Her hairbrush—with a few strands of Mia's hair still entwined in it?

At the time I had shrugged off the whole episode as a prank pulled by some idiots who couldn't stand Mia. But a voodoo doll—because that's obviously what this was—was no joking matter anymore. Sharp pins were stuck into her body. Cautiously, I pulled them all out, one at a time.

Someone hated my girlfriend.

At that moment, I heard footsteps. Quickly I slipped the doll into my pants pocket and stepped out from the shadow of the tree.

"Is something wrong? You look so serious," Mia asked.

If she ever saw that wretched thing, it would give her an enormous scare. Just like it had me.

"Nah, everything's fine." I pulled her into my arms and held her tight. I would never let anyone hurt her!

"What's gotten into you?" Mia laughed, smothered, and dug her chin into my shoulder. "It wasn't so easy to sneak out of the house," she whispered breathlessly. "My parents have been fighting again. Sounds like Mom imagined our life out here differently, somehow."

She mimicked her mother's voice: "I had hoped that we would have more time for us! For our daughter! But instead, I hardly ever see you anymore, Mark!" Mia let her head hang. I stroked her arm. She continued: "Papa couldn't understand that at all. 'Who am I busting my butt for, then?' he yelled back. 'I'm doing this for you two, for you and Mia!

So you two don't have to do without anything! Or don't you want your house in the country anymore?'"

"And what did your mother say?"

"That she'd sell the house in a minute if it would make things any better." Mia made a sound that was probably supposed to be a laugh. But instead it sounded more like a sob.

We were quiet. Only the leaves of the cherry tree rustled in the night breeze.

"Let's talk about something else, okay?" Mia finally said in a determinedly cheerful voice. "Why don't you explain why you rustled me out of my comfortable bed for a date in the middle of the night?"

I patted the backpack I was wearing and replied mysteriously, "Wait and see! It's supposed to be a surprise . . . to make up for the other night, you know."

"You don't have to apologize because you were miserable," Mia replied, almost angrily. "Everyone has tough times. You don't need to play that 'I'm a super perfect superhero' number for me, okay?"

I swallowed and nodded. Mia shoved her hand into mine and said softly, "Come on, show me your surprise."

We walked past my house and followed a narrow footpath that led us toward the river. After hiking for ten minutes, we entered the shadows of a small patch of woods right next to the water. Climbing plants grew all over the trees, smothering them with their vines. Only a little of the moon's light was able to penetrate the tangle of branches, and in spite of the flashlight I had with me, we stumbled over roots several times. The night was filled with strange noises.

More than once I thought I heard rustling and crackling behind us, as if someone were following us through the underbrush.

"Are you scared?" I asked Mia, who held my hand in a tight grip.

"No. You're here to protect me." It was so dark I couldn't even see whether she meant that ironically.

There! That rustling sound again! "Do you hear that, too?" I pointed the beam of the flashlight in the direction the sound seemed to come from. Between the vines, a pointed snout appeared and a pair of cunning yellow eyes blinked in the light.

I had to laugh. "It's just that shaggy mutt that's always following you around!"

Mia laughed, too. "Come here, dog!" she called, and it trotted toward us, wagging its tail.

"Is it much farther?" Mia groaned five minutes and dozens of mosquito bites later. She waved her arms around wildly to defend herself from the swarms of mosquitoes that were attacking us with enthusiasm. "I'm about to bleed to death here!"

"It's right around that curve," I said, hoping that was really the case.

And then, finally, we were there: we stepped out of a blackberry bramble onto a tiny, hidden, sandy beach.

Although I hadn't been here for years, nothing seemed to have changed. The narrow strip of shore sloped gently down to the river, which wound its way around a wide curve here. About thirty feet away from the bank, the black outline of the island rose above us like the prow of a large ship. Jay and I had played there when we were little kids. There had been a tree house, high up in the branches of a willow . . . my mother, her laugh like a silver bell . . . the three of us letting the sun dry us after we'd been swimming.

I hadn't been here a single time since.

Sometimes I wasn't sure what I genuinely remembered and what I had only dreamed or made up. Everything was mixed up, all jumbled and confused. Memory was like a treacherous body of water. Maybe I only remembered things I wished had happened just that way. Maybe I turned things around, distorted them without knowing it, and made them my own reality.

But no matter what had happened over there on the island, now we were in the present. This particular night everything was still and lightly touched with the silver shimmer of the full moon.

According to Wolf and his numerous female companions, this was the most romantic spot for miles around—maybe precisely because there was something disreputable about it. About a hundred years ago, the body of a drowned woman had been dragged to shore here. The old people in town claimed that occasionally you could still hear her voice wafting over the water. In spite of myself, I listened for it, and a chill ran up my spine. The sleepy rushing of the river did sound like the quiet humming of a woman.

Suddenly, I started to doubt whether it had been such a good idea to come here.

Mia, on the other hand, was completely enthusiastic. "Wow, this place is so beautiful, Alex!"

"What would you think of a little picnic?" I asked. "I brought something to eat. Bread, fruit salad . . . even a few pancakes left over from brunch this morning."

"Fabulous!" Mia's shell earrings swung back and forth jauntily. "But could we go swimming first? Or is the water not clean enough here?"

I should have told her something about dangerous salmonella and other bacteria. Unfortunately, lying has never been one of my strengths. "Uh, no, it's okay," I muttered hesitantly.

"Oh, crap!" Mia slapped her forehead. "We didn't bring bathing suits with us!" Her expression was so disappointed that I said without thinking, "It doesn't matter. No one will see us here anyway, right?"

Thin ice. Mia and I had never seen each other naked, much less slept together. For a while, Mia seemed to struggle with her modesty, but in the end she said, "Okay, but you're not allowed to look, promise?" With those words she disappeared behind a bush. Shortly thereafter, I heard the tapping of bare feet—and then a splash as Mia threw herself into the water.

When I had undressed, too, and stepped to the edge of the water, I saw her already happily paddling around. The dog sat perfectly still on the shore and didn't take its eyes off her.

"Come on in, the water's perfect!" Mia called impatiently, sending a splash in our direction. I threw the dog a resigned glance and then started to wade into the river.

Unlike my brother, who moved so gracefully in the water that he seemed to be more at home there than on land, I didn't like to swim—at least not in the river. That murky soup was kind of creepy. But I didn't want Mia to know about that.

By now, the water was up to my chest. With every step deeper, I felt the muck on the river bottom welling up between my toes. The smell of the river rose to my nose: the scent of stagnant water, fish and slightly sweet, like dead, decomposing plants . . . the smell of decay.

Something brushed against my leg, and I jumped. Reflexively, my hand felt for the small silver chain with a cross that hung around my neck. Jay had one just like it. Our grandmother insisted that we wear them all the time, for protection. Grandma's scolding voice echoed in my thoughts: "It's dangerous . . . dangerous."

It's dangerous to swim by a full moon!

Were those really the words she had said? I didn't know for sure anymore.

But then Mia came swimming over to me, and I forgot everything else. Her lips were warm and soft as she kissed me. She was so light in my arms, like a child. But her eyes were those of a woman.

I felt her naked body, her breasts against my chest, and suddenly noticed how aroused I was. I pulled her even closer to me. Her earrings tinkled quietly.

"You know those times when you feel like a piece of driftwood?" Mia asked quietly, leaning her wet forehead against mine. "I feel like that a lot. It's awful. But now, with you . . . it's better." She smiled, but as always, I sensed that vague sadness that was caught up in her smile.

Then I had an idea. "I want to show you something," I said spontaneously. "Jay and I used to do this all the time, it's a kind of game. Lie on your back."

Mia glanced at me suspiciously, but then did what I had asked. I supported her lightly at the small of her back. She was as stiff as a board, totally cramped up.

"And, what do you feel?" I asked.

"The river. The current is so strong!" Mia shuddered, and as she did, swallowed a gush of water. She quickly tried to right herself again; it was clear that she found this game strange.

"Wait! You have to breathe very calmly, that's the whole trick. Like that. . . . Now, can you feel that I'm holding on to you? Do you feel that you're not driftwood?"

"Yes," Mia whispered. Her entire body slackened in my arms as she finally relaxed. I don't know how long we floated like that in the river; I just know that I gradually started to freeze. The places where our skin touched were the only sparks of warmth in the currents of cold and darkness.

Mia's body was a hazy, milk-white silhouette. Her breasts shimmered in the water. I quickly averted my glance, but she had already noticed it. She flashed me a nervous smile, then escaped from my grip and flowed through my hands as if she were made of mercury.

"Let's see if I can make it to the island!" she called, and took off swimming as if someone were chasing her. Half disappointed, half relieved to have firm ground under my feet again, I returned to the shore. There I dried myself off with the blanket that was supposed to be for our picnic and got dressed again. In the pocket of my pants, I found the voodoo doll. I hurled the disgusting thing out into the river.

The dog sat next to me and together we watched as Mia, with quick strokes, drew closer to the spot of land surrounded by water.

"Watch out, rumor has it that the island doesn't like people!" I called out to her.

At that moment, the dog sitting next to me began to growl, a low rumble deep in its throat.

"Something just brushed against my leg!" Mia cried suddenly. "There's . . . there's something in the water, Alex!"

"It's a river. There are fish here!"

"No, it felt like . . . *hands*!" The beam from my flashlight illuminated Mia's contorted face; she was wide-eyed with fear. As fast as she could, she started to swim back toward the shore. Then I lost her again in the darkness. Had she gone under?

The dog ran back and forth along the bank, yapping like mad. Its hoarse barking sounded across the water. I wanted to jump into the river to help her, but my body didn't respond. I could only stand there and scream her name: "Mia, *MIA*!"

The dog discovered her first—with its tail wagging, it pounced on Mia, who was crawling onto the shore a few yards away from us. Panting, she dropped down in the sand, where she curled up into a ball. I draped the blanket over her shoulders and she wrapped herself up in it.

Tangled strands of hair plastered to her face. "That was not a fish, that was not a fish," she kept repeating with white lips. "What the hell was that?"

"Whatever it was, it's gone, Mia." I talked to her soothingly, trying to convince us both that she was safe now. But through the blanket, I could feel that she was still shivering. "It tried to pull me underwater, Alex!" Mia whispered insistently. "You have to believe me!" She rested her head in her hands—and stopped.

"My earrings are gone," she said in a flat voice.

"Oh. You must have lost them in the water."

"Both of them? No, I've worn them lots of times when I was swimming!" She stared at me defiantly. "Your damned fish stole my earrings!"

~~~~~

A romantic picnic in the moonlight was out of the question. Silently, we gathered up our things and headed back.

We were still a ways below the dock to our house when Mia suddenly grabbed my arm. "Look, Alex. What *is* that?" She pointed toward the river. Out there on the black water flickered tiny lights. One of them had been propelled close to the shore and had gotten caught in the tangled roots of a weeping willow right near us.

"Wait a minute, I want to have a closer look at this!" Before I could stop her, Mia had already climbed down the bank.

"And?" I asked.

Mia didn't say anything for a moment. When she finally did answer, her voice sounded astonished: "It's a kind of raft ... with a tea candle on it and a couple of ... pancakes!"

"What? Pancakes?" But her description was exactly right. Mia climbed back up again and held the thing out toward me. Incredulous, I turned it this way and that in my hands. "It looks like a kind of sacrifice," I muttered. "I've seen something like this in the pictures from my mother. People in Indonesia make offerings like this to their nature gods to win their favor."

"In case you hadn't noticed yet, we're not exactly in Indonesia!" Mia exclaimed excitedly. "So where do these sacrificial things come from?"

That question, at least, wasn't hard to answer. The closer we got to our dock, the more of these lights we discovered on the river. Without a sound, we continued on our way, as if stalking someone.

And there she was! On the dock, someone knelt and was carefully releasing another raft into the water. It was a figure in a flowing white dress, a nightgown. The hair that was usually tied back in a severe knot hung thinly over her shoulders, and her feet were bare. I had never seen her like this before . . .

It was my grandmother!

I stared at her with my mouth hanging open. Her hands moved as if she was praying the rosary, but I couldn't understand her mumbled words. I didn't understand anything anymore. While I saw Grandma pull out some metallic object and heard Mia give a muffled gasp next to me, everything seemed oddly surreal to me, as if we were caught in a nightmare.

The knife glittered in the moonlight as my grandmother cut herself in the finger and then let her blood drip into the water. "Protect this house and those who live in it," she droned in her worn-out, old woman's voice, a monotone singsong. "Accept my offering and remain in your territory, in the river!"

Grandma made the sign of the cross one last time and touched her hand to her lips. Then she turned away from the water and shuffled back up to the house with difficulty, without even looking around her.

Mia exhaled raggedly. "What on earth was that all about, Alex?" Where was my brave, calm, cool, and collected Mia? She seemed to be completely stunned. "I mean, that's . . . that's completely crazy! Why in the world is your grandmother letting her blood drip into the river by the full moon?"

I shrugged my shoulders and tried to evade her gaze.

"You know more about this than you're letting on, am I right?" Mia's voice grew louder, and she stamped the ground with a foot in a helpless rage. "Right?"

She might even have been right about that. I was afraid to think about it.

"There's something in the river, isn't there?" she whispered into my ear, as if she was afraid someone might overhear her otherwise. "What is going on here, Alex? You have to tell me!" In a subdued voice she added, "This is incredibly creepy."

I didn't tell her anything. I couldn't. Instead, I took off my silver chain with the cross and put it on Mia. My neck felt strangely cold and unprotected without its familiar presence.

"What is that?" Mia asked, looking at me with wide eyes.

"It's a substitute for your earrings. It will protect you, okay?"

She studied me for a long while. "Okay," she said finally, and then added in a slightly teasing tone, "Now I feel so much better!"

I truly wished I could have felt the same way.

≈≈≈≈≈

That night, I had bizarre dreams about water and white silhouettes. When I woke up the next morning, my pillow was damp, as if I had cried in my sleep. But I couldn't remember anything.

Chapter 12

Jay

|||||||||||||||||||||||||||||||||||||||||||||||||||||||||||||||||||||||||||||||||||||||||||||||||||||||||||||||||||||||||||||||||||||||||||||||||||

"It's strange—on these hot summer nights, everyone always pretends they're sleeping when they're actually doing something completely different," I said thoughtfully.

We were sitting next to each other leaning on the railing of the bridge, Alina and I. We spit into the river and watched as our spit blended in with the dark water flowing sluggishly beneath us.

The midday sun beamed golden from the sky, and hot wind blew through the empty streets. Other than us, there wasn't a soul outside. Even the dogs had retreated, panting into the shade.

Just one kingfisher sat an arm's length away from Alina on the railing and preened its colorful feathers. The harsh sunlight reflecting off the brilliant turquoise made me see spots. The bird would have landed on Alina's shoulder if she had wanted it to. All the animals along the river obeyed Alina.

My thoughts were still churning around the question of why people always pretended. "They're so busy pretending for each other, they don't even notice that other people have their secrets, too."

The word pleased me, so I said it out loud several more times: "Secrets, secrets, secrets." I was tickled as I thought about Grandma and Skip, both of them sitting at the breakfast table this morning with their eyes barely open, spooning up their cereal as if nothing had happened.

"I think Skip was out with Mia last night," I told Alina. "That's his girlfriend now, you know. She's really nice and . . ." Then I noticed how the sound of Mia's cello resonated in my voice, it couldn't be disguised anymore. I abruptly stopped talking, but it was already too late.

Alina had also heard the cello in me.

"So Mia is her name?" Alina drew up her lips so I could see her pale gums. "What is she doing here, anyway? She doesn't belong here!" she hissed, her voice vibrating like a string pulled too tight.

"She should get out of here, away from our river. Go back where she came from! Don't you think so, Jay?" Alina looked me directly in the eyes.

I swallowed and felt my head nodding. That's when I noticed the earrings she was wearing. "Are those . . . aren't those Mia's earrings?" I stammered. My vocal cords were tied in knots. My eyes were glued to the dangling strands of tiny shells. They jingled when Mia moved, a quiet music that always accompanied her. Seeing them on Alina now seemed wrong.

Alina smiled with satisfaction.

"You . . . you *stole* them from her!"

"She's stolen much more than that from me!"

We looked at each other for a long time, while the poplars along the shore trembled in the breeze like blazing torches.

I knew exactly what she meant, and fear grew inside me. So I said quickly, "I'll never forget you, I promise!"

"That's not enough anymore!" Alina countered. "I want you to *prove* it to me!"

"Okay, sure. How . . . what should I do?" The kingfisher that had obediently sat next to us the entire time seemed to throw me a pitying look with its beady little eyes.

"But you know already," Alina said. She made a gesture with her hand—and the kingfisher plunged down into the river like a falling jewel.

Yes, I did know. I knew it even before Alina climbed up on the railing of the bridge. It took a lot of effort to resist the impulse to cling to her bare ankles as she stood up on top of it, swaying. Alina didn't let anything or anyone hold on to her!

I knew exactly what she demanded of me.

Her image flickered before my eyes, a delicate silhouette against the blazing blue of the sky. "This . . . this is just a joke, right?" I waited for her to start laughing, but Alina's expression didn't change. "I mean, people have already landed in the hospital because of that . . . it's dangerous!" Because she didn't laugh, I did, but it sounded too shrill.

"We're going to do it together, Jay." Alina turned herself halfway toward me on the railing, as elegant as a dancer. "Do it for me!" she whispered, stretching out a hand toward me.

119

"But . . . but this is crazy!" I protested weakly, and then I had already taken hold of her hand. And then I stood next to her on the railing, trembling. I hardly dared to look down, where the water of the river yawned at least twenty feet below us. We were up so high that I didn't know how we could possibly get down from there alive.

In my head, everything was churning. The taste of bile in my mouth. "I feel sick. Please, Alina." The voice that came out of my mouth sounded peculiar, an unfamiliar whimper.

But Alina's firm grip didn't let me go. Her fingers clenched mine, foreign and as cold as stone polished by water. My limbs were clay under those fingers.

Cold sweat ran down my spine, and I shivered in spite of the heat. The wind, the whispering hot wind, pulled at me. Enticing, threatening. There were voices in the air, but I couldn't understand exactly what they were saying.

"Go!" whispered Alina.

Afterward, I couldn't say whether she pulled me with her, or I did it myself. Only one thing was certain: we jumped.

The water raced toward us. The air around me screeched. For a heartbeat, I could understand the voices more clearly; they sang of love . . . and of death.

Then we crashed onto the surface of the water. It felt as if I were being shoved through a glass wall.

Hand in hand, we sank, sank down to the muddy bottom. Alina's long hair drifted in the current like seaweed, gently brushing my face. Down here, everything was green and murky. The only thing I could recognize clearly was Alina's eyes, only a few inches away from my face.

Air bubbles streamed from my nose, tracing a shimmering path toward the surface. I wanted to follow it, to take back the air, but I couldn't. Alina had a firm hold on my wrists, holding me tight, underwater.

Slowly, I was running out of oxygen. *This isn't a game anymore! This is not fun!* I wanted to scream. Because that was the most awful thing down there: the silence. It was a stifling, deafening silence that swallowed any sounds. As if the world had gone mute; as if the world had died to me.

I tried to tear myself loose from Alina. Fleetingly, I was amazed by the sheer strength of her delicate white hands. She was much stronger than me! With my lungs burning, I fought wildly to get free, kicking, scratching her.

It was no use.

The last thing I saw was her smile, which was gradually eaten up by black holes. Then darkness.

My muscles went limp. I succumbed.

And only then did she let go of me. I shot upward through the blackness, the water's surface like a massive slab of glass, shattered as I broke through it. Air! Sounds exploded in my head.

Alina pulled me ashore.

≈≈≈≈≈

Later, we both lay in the soft grass along the shore, with Alina's hair spread out around us like a fan of silver.

"Why did you do that?" I asked. "Why did you hold on to me? It was so quiet down there, I thought I was dead already."

She took her time before she answered, all the while braiding kingfisher feathers into her hair, little slivers of heaven. "I did it so you would know how your world would be without me. Promise that you'll never forget me!"

I promised it—of course. But I couldn't take my eyes off my wrists, where her grip had left bruises like red chains.

Chapter 13

Mia

||||||||||||||||||||||||||||||||||||||||||||||||||||||||||||||||||||||||||||||||||||||||||||||||||||||||||||||||||||||||||||||||||||||||||

"Would you like some more pasta, Mia?" my mother asked. At least she was speaking to me again.

There had been an unpleasant postlude to the nighttime horror trip Alex and I had experienced recently. Just as I was about to sneak back into my room, exhausted beyond belief, the light had suddenly gone on. My mother was standing on the landing of the stairs, her lips pressed together in a tight line.

"Where are you coming from in the middle of the night? Sneaking out of the house behind our backs. Did you meet that boy from next door?" There was no more talk about the nice young neighbors.

Unfortunately, my nerves were already strained to the breaking point that night. All I wanted to do was curl up in a ball in my cozy, safe bed.

"Why don't you take care of your own problems for a change, Mom!" I had snapped back at her. When I saw the expression on her face, I was sorry I had said it. More than a week had gone by since then, and my mother was still angry.

"Thanks, but I'm full," I replied and tried to send her a conciliatory smile across the dining room table. "I'll see you later. I still have something to take care of."

≈≈≈≈≈

My stolen earrings, the bloodletting ritual, and this creature in the river . . . all of that was still haunting my thoughts. Alex apparently couldn't or didn't want to help me understand these mysterious events.

"I don't know anything about it," he said when I brought up the subject. "It may be that I used to know something, but I can't remember anymore." And he looked so tortured every time I asked that I soon left him in peace.

So I would have to get to the bottom of things myself. I had decided to play detective. This afternoon I wanted to ask Iris a few unpleasant questions.

≈≈≈≈≈

On my way to the Stonebrooks' house, I came across Jay on the dock. He seemed to be talking with someone who was hidden by the bushes. Curious, I went a little closer. But when I reached the dock, I couldn't see anyone but Jay, who was throwing stones into the water. Strange. For a moment, I thought maybe Jay was talking to himself, but that couldn't be it. That would be too crazy.

"Hi, Jay. Who were you just talking to?" I asked innocently.

He kept his gaze fixed on the river. "Alina." Another stone pierced the water's surface with a splash. Jay hurled them as if he wanted to give the river a beating.

I observed him from the side and just couldn't control my stupid tongue. "Did you two get into an argument?"

"No! Well, maybe a little." With an unusually forceful movement, Jay turned toward me and glared at me defiantly, almost with animosity. "Alina is my best friend! I'll never forget her. Never!" he added for emphasis. It sounded a little like something he had memorized.

"Okay. It's alright, I get it!" I said, astonished. Why was he reacting so strangely? Carefully, I tried to test the waters and see what else Jay might tell me: "Your friend Alina sounds like quite an interesting person. Does she go to our school?"

Jay blinked at me in confusion, as if this question had never occurred to him before. "Uh, no . . ." he replied hesitantly.

"Then she drives to a school in the city every day? That's a long way to go! I mean, she lives here in the neighborhood, right? I'd really like to meet her."

Jay suddenly seemed nervous. "I don't think that would be a good idea," he whispered into my ear so fast that his tongue almost tripped over the syllables, "because Alina doesn't like you!"

"But why not?" I exclaimed indignantly. "She doesn't even know me!"

Maybe it was just the light, but Jay's different-colored eyes seemed more noticeable to me than usual today: blue and green-brown . . .

Nervously, he looked around and whispered, "Alina is jealous. And angry, very angry!"

I opened my mouth to ask what he meant by that, but just at that moment, he touched my chest.

I froze. But Jay only touched the silver chain with the cross and twirled it in his fingers. "Ah, so *you're* wearing the chain now! Skip gave it to you, didn't he? That was clever of him. It will look out for you; that's good. It will protect you."

That's exactly what Alex had said.

"What's the necklace supposed to protect me from?" I asked with irritation. "From the shadow that leaves behind wet footprints and dead fish? Hey, stay here!"

But before I could press Jay for any more information, he had already rushed past me. As I watched him running off, it occurred to me that he had been more hunched over than usual in the past few weeks, as if something were bending his back . . .

There was something strange about this family. I was becoming more and more convinced that there was some secret that all the Stonebrooks were entangled in like an invisible web. But where was the point where all the threads came together? There had to be some kind of explanation! Even if I hadn't discovered it yet.

Maybe you should just leave this alone, whispered a warning voice inside me. But I couldn't do it. It was too late. Whatever it might be, I was already in way too deep to stop now.

I turned and walked toward the Stonebrooks' house. When you find a dead fish in your bedroom, you're entitled to a few answers.

~~~~~

I found Iris in the kitchen bent over a pot she was stirring with abandon, as if it were a magic potion. "Hello. Are you looking for Alexander?" she asked when she noticed me.

"No, um, actually I wanted to talk with you."

"Well! That's a surprise. I thought you had completely forgotten about me, old woman that I am," she said dryly, but a seldom smile brightened her face. "Have a seat, then! Would you like to try my lekvar?" And immediately she handed me her wooden spoon, completely coated with a thick, black goo. Under her expectant gaze, I had no other choice than to try it. The pungent taste of plums seasoned with cinnamon and cloves filled my mouth.

"Good, isn't it?"

"Mmmm, it's delicious!" I said. "But actually, I'm here to talk with you about something, something important."

"Yes?" Iris studied me skeptically with her eyes squinted. My courage drained away. How could I dig so deeply into family secrets here in her cozy kitchen? How could I utter a terrible suspicion about the woman whose home I was visiting?

There was a long, uncomfortable silence. Finally, I took a deep breath. "Alexander and I saw you one night not long ago at the river. There was a full moon . . ." My words hung in the air, pregnant with meaning. But no reaction!

"You . . . you dripped your blood into the water. I saw how you prayed for protection," I dared to make another stab at it. "Protection—from who, or what?"

Only the rattling of the wooden spoon broke the silence. The elderly woman had turned her back to me and stirred frantically in her pot.

"I think it still needs a little anise, don't you think so?"

I couldn't believe my ears. Alex had told me that his grandmother just kept mum about anything that didn't suit her, but that was the first time I had experienced it myself. She couldn't pretend nothing had happened! But apparently, she could. There wasn't any point in asking again. I hadn't gotten a single step closer to solving the mystery.

Frustrated, I stared at the kitchen walls covered with family photographs, where a bride and groom beamed at me happily. It was sheer mockery.

"Weren't they a beautiful couple?" Iris had stepped up behind me and gently stroked the silver frame of the picture with her fingers. That's when I recognized that it was a photo of the newly married Katarina and Eric.

Although I knew perfectly well that Iris had only guided my attention to the picture to steer me away from the unsettling topic of the blood, I was fascinated even against my will. The pregnant Katarina looked radiant in her white bridal gown embroidered with flowers.

"So there was a happy ending after all?" I asked.

"Happy ending!" she snorted, turning back to the stove with its blubbering pot of plum butter. "No, that was only the beginning. They always get it wrong in the movies. The real test isn't finding each other—it's whether they can stand everyday life together!" she declared with her spoon raised, and used the opportunity to proclaim one of her proverbs that she so often got wrong. "Marry in haste, repent at leisure! Even though they were so happy together at the beginning. We bought this house for them. And then Alexander was born not long after that. Katarina gave up her job to take care of the baby. Later Herman—my husband, may he rest in peace—and I offered to help so she could work at the photo studio again, but Eric wouldn't hear of it. He was a very proud man back then, Eric. He thought he could take care of the family himself, and that his wife shouldn't have to go to work."

Iris sighed. "I'm sure he thought he was doing her a favor. Lord knows, if it had been me, I would have been thrilled! Other women are content being wives and mothers. But not our Katarina, oh, no. She was always convinced she was destined for something greater than the rest of us. I can still hear her complaining: 'There has to be more to life than changing diapers and scrubbing the house clean, Mom!' When a letter from her friend Ruth had arrived, she would sometimes be insufferable for days afterward. Repeatedly, Katarina pestered Eric, asking if she could travel, too. The daily monotony was making her sick. Sick or not, where would the money for such foolishness come from? And then Katarina got pregnant again."

Lost in thought, Iris smiled as she filled ceramic jars with the plum butter. "Jay was an unusual child from the very first. He didn't start to talk until he was three, and he clung to Katarina's skirt hem all the time. And he only called her by her first name. After he was born, Katarina changed.

129

She seemed to finally understand that the grand trips she had always dreamed about would never happen. She turned green with jealousy! Because by then, Ruth had become a successful photographer and was traveling all over the globe.

"Dreams are dust, I always say. They only get you into trouble. But Katarina didn't want to listen to me. She had always preferred to take pictures instead of doing laundry and cooking meals. But after Jay was born, everything spun out of control. The house looked like a pigsty because she played with the children all day long. Katarina often took both of them down to the river. They would spend entire days on the island. Sometimes they even went there in the middle of the night to swim naked!" Iris admitted under her breath, as if it was embarrassing to say the scandalous word out loud.

"Of course people said the most awful things about her! I was so ashamed for her." Her wrinkled face blushed at the memory of the disgrace. "I tried to talk some sense into Katarina. But she just laughed in my face!" The elderly woman shook her head, as if she was still trying in vain to understand. "That was the first time I had the feeling that I didn't know my daughter anymore."

I waited eagerly for a continuation, but Iris fell into a brooding silence. Her watery blue eyes no longer saw me anymore but seemed to be looking into a past that had disappeared.

"There's no use. What's in the past will never return," she muttered to herself without any expression. "I think you should go home now," she said finally, pressing one of the still-warm jars of plum butter into my hands.

≈≈≈≈≈

I was lying on my bed pondering all of this when there was a knock at the door. My father stood in the doorway. "Hi, Mia. May I come in?" It wasn't very often that he made his way to my room.

"Did Mom send you? Because of my nighttime escape the other night?" I asked in a suspicious tone.

"To be honest . . . yes." We grinned at each other. The bed creaked under his weight as Dad sat down next to me. "Is it getting serious with this young man?"

"I think so," I murmured, keeping to myself that I wasn't sure if I even wanted that. The memory of Nicolas still lurked in the back of my mind, suddenly springing to the fore to push its way between Alex and me. Sometimes my past interfered with our being together so much that Alex's face, his touch, seemed to merge with those of Nicolas. And then it was all I could do to resist the urge to push Alex away.

But of course, I didn't tell my dad any of that.

His voice sounded conciliatory as he said, "We don't have anything against you getting together with Alexander. But we do want to know where you are."

"Why don't you just put one of those microchips in my ear?" I replied in a snippy tone.

"Don't be silly, Mia. You're only sixteen. Your mother and I are just concerned about you." My father tugged on his crooked tie. "I just want to ask you two to be careful as you try certain things out, you know. . . ."

I rolled my eyes. "Yeah, yeah, we had all that in sex education," I took pity on him before things got embarrassing.

"Don't worry, I won't go and get pregnant by mistake."
I thought of Katarina and shuddered inwardly.

"Oh, alright then." Relieved, my father let go of his tie
(I had been afraid he would choke himself with it). "I know
you're my big girl and will do the right thing." He looked at
me with a pride and trust in his eyes that couldn't possibly
be meant for me. I could have started bawling.

If you knew, I thought. *If you only knew . . .*

"Good, then I'll go . . ." My father seemed to hesitate,
wondering if he should give me a scratchy good-night kiss
like he used to, but then he didn't quite dare. And I didn't
dare to ask him.

≈≈≈≈≈

That night, I thought long and hard about what Iris had said.
"The first time I had the feeling that I didn't know my own
daughter anymore."

Did that happen to all parents? That they ultimately
didn't know their children at all? Can any human being
claim to truly know someone else? Did I really know Alex
and Jay, or just my image of them? The problem is that we
can only look from the outside, but the secrets are buried
deep below the surface.

Why do some secrets have to hurt so badly?

Chapter 14

Alexander

Mia and I lay next to each other on her bed and watched the play of the sun on the walls and on our skin. We tried to capture them with our hands.

In those weightless moments it was almost as if the world outside didn't exist. We were here in this light, fragile space that enclosed us like an eggshell. Where there was only the two of us.

I don't know how to explain it. The rest of the time, there was always this pull inside me, the urge to go someplace else. To the ocean, maybe. But when I was with Mia, it felt like I had arrived. Finally. As if I was exactly where I was supposed to be at that moment.

My head in Mia's lap. I had never felt so close to another person in my life.

I have no idea what demon possessed me to make me destroy that.

"Will you play something on your cello for me today, Mia?" I asked, although I knew it was stupid. But I couldn't help myself.

In the beginning, I had been curious. I tried to imagine how Mia embraced this bulky wooden thing to elicit beautiful music from it, but every time I asked her to play something for me, she put me off with some flimsy excuse: "I can't find my music," or "I'm tired, Alex—tomorrow, okay? I promise."

By now, it had become a compulsion for me to pursue it, again and again. Like some kind of test . . . of what, I didn't even know myself.

I sat upright. "Come on, Mia!" I tried again. "I'd much rather hear *you* play than listen to that classical stuff that's coming out of your CD player! What is that again?"

"'Autumn' from Vivaldi's *Four Seasons*, you buffoon!"

"Oh, right, 'Autumn,'" I mumbled.

Outside, the Indian summer bathed the days in gold in a last illusion of summer. But the nights were already cold, and in the morning, drops of dew glistened in the spiderwebs like tears.

"Alex, you know as much about music as an elephant does about tap dancing!" Mia declared, smacking me on the shoulder with her pillow—an obvious attempt to get me involved in a pillow fight. It was a hard blow, but I didn't bat an eyelash.

"Why don't you just play something for me? Maybe I could learn something!" I held her gaze defiantly. She stared right back.

Finally, Mia lowered the pillow. "Maybe later," she muttered.

"That means no, right?" My voice grew louder. I sounded like a sulky child, but I didn't care. "That means never, doesn't it, Mia?"

The crazy thing was that I wasn't even all that eager to hear her scraping and scratching around on the thing. But that wasn't the point! The core of it was that playing the cello was an important part of Mia's life. And she refused to share it with me, as if she still didn't quite trust me.

I shot a nasty look at the instrument. Gradually that red wooden box had become a symbol for everything about Mia I didn't understand. That she always pulled away from me at just the moments when we were especially close. That she didn't want to sleep with me.

The cello stood there silently, hiding its mysteries from me. I knew it was capable of producing sounds! But it remained silent. *Why?*

Sometimes I felt the urge to jump up and down on the damn *thing*, to reduce it to splinters that would reveal all. While I was still staring at the cello, disgruntled, a wave of . . . yes, *jealousy* came over me. Stupid to be jealous of a musical instrument, isn't it? But I had the feeling the cello knew Mia better than I did.

"I'm sorry, Alex," Mia's voice penetrated my dark thoughts, "I just *can't*, do you understand? It doesn't have anything to do with you!" As I looked at her sitting in front of me with her shoulders hunched and an unhappy expression stretched across her face, I just couldn't be mad at her anymore. My anger melted away and before I knew what was happening, I was apologizing to her.

"I guess I was acting like a pigheaded idiot. I don't want to force you to do anything you don't want to do. Just take as much time as you need, okay?"

I pulled her toward me and thought that everything was fine between us again. Mia let my kisses wash over her like a rain shower, without reacting. She was as still as a statue. I tried to kiss her lips warm, kiss her alive.

Her soft hair tickled my chest, and I stroked her freckled back. I kissed my favorite spot at the hollow of her neck. The skin there shimmered as translucent as the mother-of-pearl inside my shell. How delicate and soft she felt. So soft . . .

I had to think of sex and how it would be to sleep with Mia.

"But don't make me wait too long!" I whispered.

With a jolt, Mia shook me off, as if my embrace had suddenly become too suffocating for her. She stood up and went over to the window.

"What's up with you?" I asked with irritation.

But Mia just looked past me and out the window.

That was the image of her that would always stay with me in my memory: Mia there at the window, with her arms crossed in front of her breasts. Her nipples glowed red like wounds. Her face was as impenetrable as black water.

Her eyes filled with sadness.

Then Mia shook her head, and the water withdrew again. "Oh, it's nothing! I was just thinking of something."

≈≈≈≈≈

Later on, I saw this scene play out in my head over and over again. I wish I could have pressed the stop button like the one on Jay's recording device, rewound, and done everything over again. And done it right this time. *Please, Mia, talk to me! I can tell something is bothering you! You don't need to play the superwoman for me—what's going on?*

There were so many opportunities to ask! I should never have given up. Instead, I let myself be content with that meaningless answer.

Was it cowardice? Was it just easy and comfortable? Did I not want to start up another fight right after we'd made up? Whatever the reason, it doesn't matter anymore. There's no rewind button in life.

The one thing that's certain is that I didn't keep asking, even though I had felt that something was deeply wrong all along. I wasn't there for Mia when she needed me.

And so our summer passed. Irretrievably. The first wilted leaves were already being carried away on the surface of the river like extinguished gold sparks.

Did I already sense how close autumn was? Maybe. Because I do remember looking out the window and wishing I could magically put all the cherries back on the branches of our tree.

~~~~~

In that night, I dreamed of Mia. In my dream, her body was a red cello. She plucked her strings and sang, but I couldn't hear a sound, no matter how hard I tried.

"Sing louder, Mia! I can't understand you!" I called.

And then she started to cry. The tears running down her face became a powerful flood that carried her away, still singing silently. Away from me.

I ran alongside the river, waved, screamed her name. But she moved farther and farther away, relentlessly . . . she got smaller and smaller until she disappeared into the gray horizon.

And I was left behind on the shore.

Second Intermezzo

My memories of sunny, golden summer days have left me. Probably frozen. Just like the dreams of a marvelous rescue. Maybe I just dreamed up my entire life, and this hole in the ice is the only true reality. It's as if I were dissolving. All that's still left of me is this tough strand of life that stubbornly clings to a jagged edge of ice. Like ivy on a stone.

My fingertips are already completely numb. I can feel how my blood is gradually flowing more slowly, as sluggish as the river, until it finally freezes into ice, too. Do I still have feet? I don't feel them anymore. I don't feel anything anymore. Just cold, cold all the way through to my heart . . .

I know the river will win in the end! Its black water laps at me; I feel the gentle, inevitable tug of the current that wants to pull me under the ice. Like strong, dark hands. Stronger than me . . .

Dully, I stare at a wilted leaf that's trapped in the reflecting ice in front of me and think that that's my future.

I broke our blood oath. Nothing can save me now.

Soon, very soon, I'll have to let go. Then I'll slowly sink down to the bottom in a cloud of air bubbles. Down to the fish, where it's dark and quiet.

I'm not even afraid anymore. By now, it almost doesn't matter. I'm so tired. I just want to sleep . . . dangerous, I know, but . . . I can't do it anymore.

Sleep. Let me finally sleep.

L'AUTUNNO
AUTUMN

Chapter 15

Jay

||||||||||||||||||||||||||||||||||||||||||||||||||||||||||||||||||||||||||||||||||||||||||||||||||||||

The calls of migrating birds drove a wedge in the blue October sky. All around us the trees rustled their last autumn songs before the sap solidified in their trunks and they sank into a long, cold silence.

I captured everything with my recorder, all of this red and gold burning above our heads. But now I could only think what a waste it was that no one but Alina and I got to see this beauty. Just yesterday, Mia had asked me again when I would finally take her to the island. Oh, how badly I wanted to show her everything! The field and my music castle and . . .

"What are you thinking about, Jay?" Alina looked at me with her head tilted to the side.

"Oh, nothing special," I said quickly. "I don't feel very good today."

"Well let's see if we can cheer you up a little!" Alina replied, and gave a warbling call. A moment later, a kingfisher fluttered onto her shoulder with a strip of flapping silver in its beak. Alina took the bird's catch away from it, held the little fish by the tail, leaned her head back—and swallowed it whole, just like the herons do.

I wanted to look away, but I couldn't. I stared at her with reluctant fascination.

Alina casually wiped her mouth with a hand and grinned at me. "You'd like to be able to do that, too, wouldn't you, Jay? The kingfishers are calling."

The bird on her shoulder sparkled so beautifully in the sunlight. I stretched my fingers out to touch it, and then pulled my hand back again. "I would like to," I admitted hesitantly, "but I can't. I mean, you're their queen! The queen of the kingfishers . . . and I'm just Jay."

Alina graced me with a smile that sparkled like fish scales. "We're much more alike than you think, Jay," she answered gently. "Believe me, I could teach you a melody that would bend the tips of the willows to the earth. You could make the river spill over its bank and much more, if only you wanted to."

Her talk was making me nervous. "But that . . . that's not possible!" I contradicted her, confused.

"Who says that?"

"Well, everyone! Grandma, Skip, my teachers . . ."

"What do *they* know?" Alina hissed. "They cling to their pathetic rules and 'scientific definitions!'" She practically spit out the words. "Those idiots don't know a thing about real life! And nothing about the river!" Alina lowered her voice to a conspiratorial whisper that wound its way into my ear. "The only thing that matters is what *we* want, Jay. That and nothing else makes our reality! Go ahead, try it!" she commanded. "Try to call the bird to you."

Obediently, I stretched out my hand. It wasn't going to work, anyway. And sure enough, the kingfisher didn't ruffle a feather!

"You have to concentrate!" Alina insisted impatiently.

I *was* trying—really hard. Beads of sweat broke out on my forehead. Every thought in my head droned *come, come here*.

There! With choppy beats of its wings, like a wound up toy, the kingfisher slowly made its way toward me . . . and landed on my palm! At first, I was afraid its metallic blue would cut my fingers. But it was so soft. Its tiny claws tickled my skin, and I felt its feather-light heft in my hand. A bundle of fluff. A quivering little bit of life.

I could crush it between my fingers, if I wanted to . . . just like that. I knew it, and the bird knew it, too.

"Do it!" Alina whispered, as if she had read my thoughts. Her eyes were green-brown and unfathomable, just like the river. As if the river flowed through them.

I didn't know if she was serious. Was this supposed to be another one of her crazy tests, where I had to prove something to her? Did Alina want me to kill the bird for her?

My left eye, the brown one, began to tear up. Was the river perhaps in me, too? My fingers twitched. *You could make the river spill over its bank, you could . . .*

"No," I said, uncurling them again. "I don't think I want to!" Then I raised my hand. "Fly, little one!"

But only after Alina had released the dazed bird with a trill did it take off. Every beat of its wings announced its relief at having escaped death once again. *To be alive!*

Alina watched it go with a strange smile. As if she had just confirmed something she had suspected for a long time. I had no idea if I had passed her little test or not. But I sensed that something would happen. Soon.

My recording device was still running and recorded the silence between us. I turned it off.

≈≈≈≈≈

After Alina had left, this horrible feeling overcame me, as if a small animal were gnawing away at my insides. It ate into my heart. I listened carefully to my heartbeat and it sounded dull and hollow. Like rain on a fall day.

When I tried to raise the corners of my mouth in a smile, I couldn't manage it. It was hard to breathe, and I was dizzy. Something was wrong with me! Maybe I was getting sick. As fast as I could, I rowed for home.

Grandma wasn't there, but instead I found my big brother. "I think I'm sick, Skip," I groaned weakly. "Measles, at least."

First, he hustled me into the bathroom and stuck a thermometer in my mouth. "Hmm," he grunted meaningfully, like our doctor, when he removed it again. "Well, you don't have a fever. And you don't look especially sick, either. Tell me exactly what's wrong."

"It's as if I'm suffocating." I didn't know how I should explain it to him. "I'm getting heavier and heavier, and I'm drowning in sadness."

Skip observed me with an expression on his face that I couldn't understand. Then he suddenly hugged me tightly. He never did that! "Better?" he asked a little awkwardly and let go.

I took a moment to think about how I felt. "Yeah," I nodded, astonished, "a little."

"What you have is something everyone has to deal with some time or another," Skip explained to me. "Could it be that you feel a little lonely, Jay?"

At first, I wanted to contradict him. Loneliness was something for other people, nothing that had anything to do with me. I had Alina, after all. But then I had to admit that Skip was probably right. I didn't have the measles. I was lonely.

"Welcome to the world of mere mortals, little brother!"

"It feels awful, and I want it to go away! What makes it better?" I asked.

"You just need a girlfriend. You'll see, it helps!" Skip said and grinned to himself. He was surely thinking about Mia.

A girlfriend . . . but I already had Alina, didn't I? I dragged myself upstairs to my room to listen to some of the recording from this afternoon. If girlfriends were the cure, maybe Alina's voice would help me. After all, without meaning to, I had recorded our conversation earlier.

As I quickly rewound the tape, all the voices sounded like the twittering of birds. Then I played the recording at normal speed.

But the only voice to be heard on the recording was mine—and the cries of the kingfishers.

Chapter 16

Mia

⁣||||||||||||||||||||||||||||||||||||||||||||||||||||||||||||||||||||||||||||||||||||||||||||||||||||||||||||||||||||||||||||||||||||||||||||

The stray dog barked in protest when I left him behind on the shore. "I'll be back soon!" I called to my dog, and then our boat was already gliding out onto the river.

"Why are you taking me to your island today, after you've done everything you could to avoid it for so long?" I asked Jay, who sat on the bench across from me.

"I just couldn't stand it anymore," he muttered, and for a brief moment, I felt guilty for pestering him so much.

But only for a moment. A gust of wind rippled the water and opened gaps in the layers of clouds above us, revealing patches of blue sky.

I enjoyed the sun's rays on my face as I observed Jay. The river seemed to give him confidence. As awkward as he so often was everywhere else, his rowing strokes were rhythmic and elegant. The oars seemed to skim the surface of the water, like the beating of a bird's wings. We were practically flying, drawing closer to the mysterious island.

And then there it was in front of us—an elongated strip of land, like the spine of a crouching predator. The trees along its banks were aflame in spectacular shades of gold and red.

Jay skillfully maneuvered the boat to the island, jumped onto land, and tied the boat to a tree. The whole time I was so excited I could hardly sit still. But now, just before getting out, I felt a warning, prickling sensation on my neck. A few weeks ago—just a few yards from this very place—I had almost been drowned.

I had to think of all the creepy stories people in town told about this place. Uncomfortable, I stared over at the shore. The yellow leaves of the trees seemed to stare back like thousands of eyes.

I suppressed the nervous impulse to chew on my fingernails. "What if the island doesn't like me?" I asked.

Jay laughed. "Of course the island likes you! *I* like you!" Impatiently, he gestured for me to get out. It was probably silly, but I still had a strange feeling.

"Hey, Jay . . ." I stalled, "what does your friend Alina think about you bringing me here? I mean, it's kind of your island. She seems to not like me at all—though I still don't get why."

Alina is jealous. And angry, very angry. Jay's remark echoed in my head. Then the image of the dead fish in my room. And the broken cello strings.

Could this Alina have something to do with that? Whoever had done it—what else might he or she be capable of?

"I don't want Alina to get even more pissed off at me because I'm poking around her island," I murmured.

Jay wasn't laughing anymore. "This is *my* island, too!" he said defiantly. "And *I* invited you! It's none of Alina's business!"

He stretched out a hand toward me to help me. I hesitated. Then I grasped it.

My shoes immediately sank into the wet, spongy layer of fallen leaves that covered the ground. It was odd to imagine that I was probably the first stranger to set foot on this island in a long, long time. I felt like an explorer, someone stranded on a faraway island.

A colorful bird perched on a branch near the shore heightened the foreign, exotic impression. It studied us with its black beady eyes without the slightest shyness—as if it wanted to greet us.

"Oh, look, Jay!" I cried with excitement. "Is that a kingfisher? I've never seen a real one!"

Jay froze when he saw the bird. And then his face contorted with an expression of rage that I had never seen before. "Get out of here! Leave me alone!" he screamed, throwing a piece of bark at it. The bird fluttered away in a cloud of shimmering turquoise-blue feathers and disappeared in the brush.

"Why did you chase it away?" I yelled at Jay angrily. "It was a harmless little bird."

"It was a spy!" Jay muttered through clenched teeth. There was definitely something wrong with this guy. Shaking my head, I followed him through the undergrowth.

The island was larger than I had surmised from the water. Countless pale violet flowers bloomed among the tree trunks. Were they some kind of crocus? I wanted to pick one, but Jay stopped me. "Don't touch them!" he warned. "Those are meadow saffron. They're poisonous!"

I quickly pulled my hand away, and we continued.

The sea of flowers all around us gave me a surreal impression of springtime, even though the leaves had already fallen from many of the trees. It was if time took a different course here and didn't obey the usual laws of nature.

Jay had once called it the Island of Bliss. Yes, I could feel it. This island was a strange, magical place . . .

The wind had gathered strength and rustled through the fallen leaves. Single leaves fell and rocked to the ground at a majestically slow pace, back and forth, seeming to defy gravity itself—like sparks of gold. I followed them with my eyes, not sure if I was awake or dreaming. There seemed to be a tinkling and clanging hovering in the air, or did that only exist in my head?

"Do you hear that, too?" I asked, and Jay smiled and nodded. It actually seemed like we were drawing closer to the source of the sounds; they were getting louder, clearer.

We stepped into a small clearing. "What is that?" I whispered.

In the middle of the clearing stood a huge, bizarre tree. I think it was a willow. Its branches were knotted and twisted around each other, and its leaves rustled in the wind. And the tree *sang* for us!

Jay touched the rough bark as if he were greeting an old friend. I thought he might be reaching to hug the tree when Jay suddenly grabbed a rope ladder that I hadn't noticed before. Jay climbed up skillfully, and with a big grin gestured to me from above that I should follow him. I climbed up after him, high into the crown of the tree.

At the place where the enormous trunk forked, there was a wooden platform with a crooked railing. I looked around in astonishment with my eyes, and ears, wide open. Now I finally understood where the music was coming from!

Surrounding us on all sides in the branches, a curtain of rusted forks chimed as they jangled against each other. Carved pieces of wood clapped melodically. Directly above us, a large mobile made from beach finds—glass bottles, a rusted cowbell, and all kinds of other flotsam—twirled delicately in the steadily increasing wind. It was like a polyphonic, ethereal orchestra playing a chaotic melody that only Jay knew and directed.

"Welcome to my musical castle! Do you like it?" he asked quietly.

"It's unbelievable!" I stammered. "Did you make all this yourself?"

Jay nodded, beaming with pride. Solemnly, he announced, "And now I'll sing for you."

Jay's singing voice was surprisingly low. His "song" had neither a continuous melody nor a text I could understand. It was simply a melodic rising and falling of his voice of sustained vowels that combined into a strange and fantastic language: "Aaaaoooooo uuuuiiiii . . ."

Jay rocked back and forth, almost as if he had fallen into a trance. His full concentration seemed to be focused on a point inside him, like beams of light by a magnifying glass until flames suddenly erupt. The whole thing felt something like a ritual ceremony—a little creepy!

What was that? At first, I thought it was just the clanging of the mobile in the background, but then. . . . Every fiber of my body strained to listen. Goose bumps crept up my back like cold fingernails.

And then there was a second voice, hovering above Jay's rumbling bass! A voice vibrating as crystal clear as a glass harp and much higher than Jay's!

"What is it, Mia?" Jay had stopped singing and leaned toward me, clearly concerned.

"I'm alright," I murmured, but my fingers were trembling. Jay took my hands in his and breathed on them until they were steady. He probably thought I was cold. He was sweet. Why in the world, with all the nice guys out there, did I have to get involved with a jerk like Nicolas? If I hadn't fallen for him, of all people, everything probably would have turned out completely differently.

Jay's face was suddenly very close to mine. He looked just as uncertain and fragile as I felt. We both held our breath . . .

And then he kissed me. Or I kissed him.

It was different than with Alex. And entirely different than with Nicolas. Jay's lips were warm and soft and so wonderfully awkward that I was sure he had never kissed a girl before.

Kissing him was like kissing for the first time. I left the memory of Nicolas behind me—shed it like a dirty old shell. It was as if I were kissing myself free of him. Jay gave me back my innocence; he let me have his, generously, and without any strings attached.

Slowly, we separated from each other. Turmoil churned inside me. I didn't know if I should laugh or cry. I had just kissed my boyfriend's brother!

"What was *that*?" I stuttered.

"It was a kiss," said Jay with a blissful grin. Even a blind person would have noticed that he was completely infatuated with me.

I had to laugh. This was all so surreal. Fortunately, Jay didn't take offense, but started giggling along with me. I loved that about him: you could just do what you felt moved to do, no matter how crazy it seemed. With Jay, I never had to be afraid of doing something wrong. That was probably the reason I enjoyed his company so much, and why I had even let him watch me play my cello.

But even as our laughter faded, I knew instantly that *I* wasn't in love with *Jay*. And strangely enough, for the very same reasons! I was able to trust Jay implicitly because I didn't take him entirely seriously. In my eyes, he was still half a child. Harmless.

Our kiss had been lovely—but something was missing. Something like passion. Jay couldn't be dangerous for my heart.

But somewhere deep down, I suspected that people could only get truly close to each other if they were willing to risk something. If something isn't a little bit dangerous for your heart, it can't make it sing either, can it?

And the person who could make such chaotic feelings swirl around in my heart wasn't Jay—it was Alex.

"Uh, Jay, I don't know what just came over me," I stammered, bright red with embarrassment. I didn't want to hurt him, but we had to set things straight right away. "I'm going out with Alex, and I don't want to ruin things with him. I don't want you to have any false hope."

"Shhh!" Jay placed his finger on my lips. "I know you're in love with Skip. But please don't say you regret that kiss! *I'm* not sorry it happened!" he said thoughtfully. "It was nice . . . a little scary." Jay smiled a little wistfully, with bewilderment. "Grown up, I think."

We sat next to each other in peaceful silence, captivated by the fragile intimacy between us. We both knew there would be no second kiss. All we had was this moment.

And then it was gone, carried away by the cool breeze. We were back to normality. The wind had grown stronger and made us shiver. "I think a storm is blowing in," Jay said, as if he was taking care to find his way back to a harmless topic. *As if we're in a bad movie*, I thought to myself, *now we're talking about the weather*!

But then I looked up at the sky and registered with shock how unbelievably fast it had clouded over. The threatening sky was a dark, surreal gray-blue, just the color of a storm.

Its harbingers were already tugging at my clothes and making my hair fly around my face. I spit a strand out of my mouth. "Do you feel how the tree is swaying, Jay?"

In that moment, a fierce gust of wind whipped through the branches of the musical castle. It made the big mobile above our heads sing with furious angels' voices. I looked up and saw how the fragile construction reeled in the wind, tipping to one side as its balance was disturbed. Then the mobile crashed down onto us!

It would have landed right on top of me if Jay hadn't sensed it and pushed me aside at the last second. We fell on top of each other on the wooden board of the tree house as shards of glass rained down all around us.

"Come on, let's get out of here!" Jay called above the howling of the storm, pulling me up. As fast as our feet could move, we climbed down the rope ladder. Then we ran hand in hand through the forest, carelessly trampling the meadow saffron, whose blossoms seemed to turn toward us like blind heads.

The boat, where was the boat? My sides ached, but Jay relentlessly urged me onward. Thorny vines tore at us like greedy hands, as if they were trying to hold us back. They scratched our skin.

The pain of the scratches is what made me realize that this was really happening. It was as if I were waking up from a deep dream. And suddenly, I was scared! I could see in Jay's eyes that he felt the same way.

The trees groaned under the force of the storm. All around us, leaves and twigs spattered to the ground, as if an invisible person were shaking the branches in outrage. But there, up ahead—wasn't that where we had left the boat? Yes, there it was! Finally! I almost sobbed with relief.

Jay sped up.

The last thing I remembered about the island was the kingfisher. In the midst of the tumultuous chaos, it perched on a branch near the shore in complete calmness and stared at us as we moved away. Its eyes were as cold as death.

Chapter 17

Alex

||||||||||||||||||||||||||||||||||||||||||||||||||||||||||||||||||||||||||||||||||||||||||||||||||||||||||||||||||

It stormed and rained almost without interruption for three days. Then came the flood. I could see it from the window of my room when I got up on that gray Saturday morning.

The bushes along the riverbank stood in muddy water and stretched their bare branches to the sky as if they were drowning. The first channels of overflowing water had already begun to lap at our yard with thirsty tongues. Of course, I had often seen our peaceful little stream transform itself into an entirely different, raging torrent, but never in such a short time. If this kept going, we would need to start stacking sandbags around our house soon.

I stared at the churning mass of water outside. It was the color of congealed blood . . .

. . . *congealed blood, what nonsense!* I shook my head energetically. That strange color was due to all the clay being stirred up by the river, of course. A perfectly harmless explanation. Grandma was slowly making me crazy, too, with her nervous fussing. For days now, she had been creeping through the house muttering ominous phrases under her breath. "The spirit of the river is displeased. That's going to bring us bad luck, terrible bad luck!"

I shrugged my shoulders and slipped into my clothes. Muffled snoring came from Jay's and Dad's bedrooms, but I was already hungry for breakfast. I headed down the stairs.

"Grandma?"

No answer. Not a sound. Not even the dry clicking of her rosary beads. She must be in the kitchen, praying to her holy Magda—or whichever of those saints is responsible for floods, I thought. Apparently, Grandma didn't see the slightest contradiction in being a strict Catholic and at the same time believing in superstitious garbage like river spirits.

A cool breeze greeted me as I stepped into the kitchen. The door to the terrace stood wide open and creaked quietly as the wind moved it back and forth.

Only after I closed the door did I notice the footprints.

With a feeling of dread that I couldn't even explain to myself, I stared at the wet footprints on our wooden floor. I had to think of the tracks in our vegetable garden that Mia always talked about—of a shadow that left behind dead fish and voodoo dolls.

Now it had come inside our house. An invisible boundary had been crossed. What did it mean?

The old fears crept out of the cracks in the floor where they had been hidden for years. And with them, the memory of something I had banished to the deepest recesses of my memory. The awareness that something was out there. Something that spied on me and followed me wherever I went. It had only been glimpsed out of the corners of my eyes, but no matter how fast I turned around, I could never identify it.

I noticed I was breathing faster. The tightness in my chest grew, and with it the certainty that something dangerous was brewing over us. Jay, Mia, and me. Like a threatening cloud, it overshadowed our lives.

Don't flip out, man! I noticed that I was close to hyperventilating and forced myself to take deep, calm breaths.

Gradually, I could think more clearly again. I crouched down to take a closer look at the footprints.

They were small and dainty, like the feet of a girl or young woman. But what crazy person still ran around barefoot in November? And most puzzling of all, what was she doing in our kitchen?

My eyes followed the tracks, which led from the terrace door to the back wall of the kitchen. I froze, blinking twice. But when I opened my eyes again, it was still there: something was smeared on our once-so-white walls in red-brown paint. The giant red letters seemed to dance around before my eyes, taunting me. Finally, I saw what was written there.

TRAITOR!

Who . . . what the hell? The fine hairs on the back of my neck stood straight up.

I dragged my father and my brother out of their beds. Now all three of us were standing in front of the smeared wall and staring at the scrawled letters.

"Well, boys," Dad scratched his stubbly chin, baffled. "Are you two in some kind of trouble I should know about?" he asked sternly. I shrugged my shoulders, and my gaze involuntarily darted over to Jay. My brother had dark rings under his eyes, as if he hadn't slept. As soon as he had seen the writing, he had drawn his shoulders up, as if he were suddenly freezing.

As if he knew perfectly well that the message was intended for him.

But he pressed his lips together as our father continued his questioning. "Is this some stupid stunt your buddies pulled? Have you been fighting with someone?"

Silence.

Dad sighed. "Either way—get rid of this mess, or your grandmother will have a heart attack when she gets home from church! I'm going back to bed for a few minutes." Sleeping in on Sunday mornings was sacred to him, so he trudged off toward his bedroom. At the bottom of the stairs, Dad stopped again and grumbled, "Maybe it would be better to lock the doors from now on." Was I imagining things, or was there a touch of worry in his voice?

The wooden steps protested under our father's weight. As soon as the creaking was quiet again, I turned to Jay. "So what's going on?"

He tried to play innocent. "What do you mean? What should be going on?" But his eyes gave him away. His two-colored gaze wouldn't meet mine but darted all over the room like an animal caught in a trap. "It's nothing, Skip. Everything is okay," he assured me.

First Mia, and now my brother was starting to be secretive, too. They were driving me crazy. "Oh, come on, Jay!" I said with irritation as I looked for a scrub brush under the kitchen sink. When I finally found one, I had a great desire to throw the thing at his thick skull. "For days you've been holed up in your room, even though Grandma usually has to tie you to a chair to keep you from roaming around by the river!"

"In case you hadn't noticed, the weather's been awful," Jay retorted snottily, as he filled a bucket with soapy water.

I laughed derisively. "As if that had ever stopped you before!" For a while, I watched him as he grimly scrubbed the wall. What I had thought was paint at first turned out to be river mud, thick with clay. No matter how much Jay scoured, the stuff wouldn't come off; reddish streaks marred half of our kitchen wall, and again I was reminded of blood.

Finally, Jay put the brush down, exhausted, and leaned his head against the wall. His pale legs poked out of his too-short pajama pants like thin sticks. For some reason, I felt sorry for him.

"Sit down, you blockhead. I'll make us some tea. And then you'll tell me everything, alright?" I grumbled. Jay hesitantly sat down at the kitchen table and rubbed his ice-cold feet against each other.

When I opened the cabinet to take out two mugs, I found the dragonflies. They were perched like extra handles on Grandma's rose-patterned china. "Damned bugs!" I resisted the impulse to wave my arms around my head wildly when the startled insects almost flew into my face. With an aggressive buzzing, they whirred around in our kitchen like metallic flashes. "Shouldn't they have gone to sleep for the winter a long time ago?" I protested, shooing them out the window. Nature was all topsy-turvy.

"Everything is going haywire here lately! Yesterday flies hatched and crawled out of my cornflakes! Freaking flies, can you imagine, Jay? I almost threw up, it was so disgusting! And now this crap!" I pointed accusingly at the smeared wall. "I have no clue what's going on here, Jay—but I'd bet my life that you know!"

I slammed his cup down on the table in front of him and the tea splashed over the top. "Whatever it is—it has to stop, do you understand!" I spluttered. Only in my thoughts, I added . . . *because it's starting to scare me!*

But maybe my brother heard it anyway—he could do things like that sometimes. And finally he opened his mouth.

"It's hard to explain, Skip," he said evasively. "It's like this . . ."

And just then, at the worst possible moment, there was a knock on the door to the terrace. Jay was so startled he jumped like an electric shock had jolted through his body. But it was only Mia.

Her reddish-brown hair was curled from the dampness, or from excitement. "Hi, Alex," she gushed. "I'm sorry to burst in so early in the morning, but you have to help me . . ."

Suddenly, she spied my brother at the kitchen table and broke off. "Oh, hi Jay."

Jay turned as red as a freshly picked cherry. If it had been anyone other than my awkward little brother, I would have sworn that . . .

162

"What am I supposed to help you with?" I asked. Mia seemed to have lost her train of thought.

"Um, right . . . it's about the dog. You know, the stray that always follows me around. Recently he's even been letting me pet him," she added. There was a noticeable note of pride in her voice. "But now he's been missing for two days, just disappeared, as if he's been swallowed up by the earth. That's never happened before, and I'm starting to worry about the lousy mutt," Mia said sheepishly. "Maybe he got run over by a car and is lying around somewhere hurt. . . . I wanted to ask if you'd maybe help me look for him."

"I can help, too!" Jay called in the background. "I just need to get dressed." Before I could stop him, he had already bounded up the stairs, obviously relieved to escape a serious discussion with his big brother, at least for now.

"You're not getting out of this—we'll talk later!" I called after him. Mia turned to me with a questioning expression.

"It's nothing. Of course I'll help you look!" I assured her quickly and went to put on my tennis shoes. In the left shoe was a big toad. It looked up at me with knowing, golden eyes—and jumped away with a croak. Mia laughed. I didn't.

≈≈≈≈≈

After three hours of fruitless searching in a misty rain, Mia and I returned to the house, exhausted and chilled to the bone. Although we had combed the entire area, we hadn't seen a single clue about the fate of the stray dog, not even a hair.

Mia seemed defeated, and her damp curls sagged sadly. "We can try again tomorrow," I tried to cheer her up. "The old mutt will show up again soon, you'll see. He's probably curled up in the bushes somewhere, having too much fun letting us look for him."

She looked at me, then she took my face in both hands and kissed me passionately, as if she had something to make up for.

"Wow. What was that for?" I asked when I could catch my breath again.

"To thank you for being you."

I wanted to tell her how important she was to me, how much I loved her. The three magic words were on the tip of my tongue, but Mia put a finger to my lips. Her smile, so familiar and yet so inscrutable, was the last I saw of her before she disappeared into the gray rain.

Chapter 18

Jay

Twilight fell early in the gray November sky, getting caught in the bare branches of the willows. I had been tramping around the area for hours in search of Mia's dog, mainly to postpone the coversation with Skip. But by now, I was so cold that I didn't care about anything. I just wanted to go home. Still, it was a mistake to take the shortcut along the riverbank. As I walked along looking at the seething high water, out of the corner of my eye, I suddenly noticed a figure in front of me on the narrow path. I almost ran right into her.

"Oh . . . Alina!" My heart skipped a few beats and then fluttered hectically against my chest like a bird with a broken wing. Ever since my visit to the island with Mia, I had done everything in my power to avoid Alina. I had no idea how much she knew, or how angry she was . . .

"Sorry, I don't have time for you right now," I stammered.

But Alina didn't make the slightest move to let me pass her. "I think you do," she replied calmly, staring right at me.

In spite of the damp, cold air, I was sweating. I tried to tell my body there was no reason to be afraid. It was Alina, after all. But my bird-heart was doing flips and not paying any attention to me, and my legs would have liked to run away.

I swallowed. "This morning in our kitchen . . . the writing on the wall . . . and the animals. That was you, wasn't it?" I asked. "You can't do things like that, do you hear? Skip is already getting suspicious. You're making a mess of everything!"

"Me? *You're* the one ruining everything, Jay! *Traitor*!" Her voice tore the awful word into my skin, with red letters that burned. "You brought that Mia to our island! You even sang for her . . . you *kissed* her!"

Kissed! Alina's voice sounded brittle, like when you break a glass. Had the kingfisher told her that? Had she been looking through its pearl eyes? At any rate, she knew everything and there was no point in lying. But I didn't want to tell anymore lies anyway. A wild defiance welled up in me: that was my business alone, for me, Jay, alone to decide. Not Alina!

"I can kiss whoever I want!" By now, my heart was beating so loudly I could hardly hear my own words.

"Oh, our little one is getting defiant!" Alina hissed. She wore her placid face like a cracked mask now, with something foreign and frightening lurking behind it. I sensed it, her icy rage that almost froze the air between us.

"You probably think you don't need me anymore; you want to just trade me in for a new girlfriend! Do you have any idea what that means? Without me, you'll become just

166

like everyone else: dependent on others, vulnerable, *weak*. A pathetic prisoner of your emotions!"

Alina's laugh stabbed me in the chest like a glass knife. "Just look at you, Jay, it's already started. You've fallen for this Mia, haven't you? Even though you know she's your brother's girlfriend! Even though you know you can't have her!"

The world blurred before my eyes. I wanted to turn away, but Alina held my face tightly between her hands. "My poor, Jay," she said in a velvety voice, catching my tears with her beautiful, cold fingers. Then she put them in her mouth and sucked on them. "Salt," Alina murmured. "Your tears never tasted salty before." She looked at me with disbelief. "Is *this* really what you want to trade me for, Jay? Salt and heartache? Look at me and answer me!"

"I . . . I don't know . . ." I stammered, twisting under her grip. "Please, let me go. I don't have time for this now. I have to help Mia look for her dog!"

"Oh, the dog. I don't think you'll find him!" Alina giggled as if she had just made a joke that only she could understand.

"Why not?" I asked hesitantly. Even as I asked the question, I had a feeling that I wouldn't want to hear her answer.

"Well, the dog went for a little swim, you know?" Alina placed her forehead against mine, sending me her thoughts. For a heartbeat, I had a clear image of the dog. He would never eat chocolate-covered raisins again. His blue, swollen tongue hung out of his mouth; his eyes were empty and broken.

It was like a sucker punch. I jerked back from Alina, staggered, and fell in the mud. "You . . . you're . . ." I whispered. I was so appalled I couldn't find the words as I slid away from her backward on the seat of my pants. "Mean and . . . gruesome, that's it! How could you do such a thing?"

"I do what I want! I'm the queen of the kingfishers," Alina replied, tossing back her head. But her voice sounded uncertain this time. She had wanted to intimidate me, punish me for my disloyalty. But she hadn't counted on such a strong reaction from me. I think it scared her.

"A dead stray, who cares about that? Come back to me, Jay. Come back to the river!"

I shook my head. "No. I don't want to be like you!" With effort, I scrambled to my feet. "I'd rather be a crying human being with a heart than a kingfisher with a heart of ice," I said quietly. Then I turned around and walked away. Away from her.

I had only gone a few steps when I heard her call: "Jay, wait! I'm sorry! Don't go away, do you hear me?" Alina begged me. I closed my ears.

But I could still hear it: the raw heartbeat of her fear. Her pain, her rage, her astonishment that I dared to turn away from her. All of that echoed in my body.

"Please, don't do this! Don't leave me. You can't do this! You promised me!" Alina screamed now. "I CAN'T EXIST WITHOUT YOU, JAY!"

I wasn't entirely sure if I could live without her, but I yelled back, "I don't ever want to see you again! Do you hear me, Alina? I'm forgetting you! I'm forgetting your name! You're dead to me! Dead and forgotten!"

My feet were so heavy. Everything had become so heavy. But maybe that's the way it has to be when you suddenly carry the weight of your life on your own shoulders.

≈ ≈ ≈ ≈ ≈

When I got home, Grandma looked at me with a strange expression on her face. She insisted that I go lie down for a while.

"Your brother isn't feeling well, Alexander. So leave him alone for a while." Skip slinked around me like a cat around a dish of milk, but she firmly shooed him away. I could see the questions burning on the tip of his tongue as Grandma slammed my bedroom door in his face.

I let her cover me up. "What on earth happened?" she asked.

"Oh, Grandma, I feel so strange. As if something in me has died." She muttered something I couldn't understand and brought me a cup of hot milk with honey in bed, and her rosary. I didn't touch either one of them.

Time passed. The time after Alina. I dozed with open eyes. Suddenly, a muffled bang made me sit bolt upright. It sounded as if someone had flung something against my window.

Slowly, I stood up and dragged myself over to the window to look out. Down on the ground I saw something blue shimmering.

I stormed down the stairs and outside. It was the kingfisher. Its neck was broken. The little body, still warm, hung lifeless in my hand. Already ashes, dirt.

I knew what that meant. The bird was a message to me: Alina was trying to get to me, even if she had to send her bleeding minions through panes of glass to do it. She was demanding me back like a lost object she had a fundamental right to.

You belong to me, you'll always belong to me, whether you want to or not, said the dead bird. *I'll never let you go, never!*

Yes, I knew what that meant: from now on, there would be war between Alina and me.

Later, I buried the kingfisher beneath the branches of Grandma's lilac bush. I cried as the dirt fell on its wings and the black crumbs swallowed up its glistening blue.

That night, even the rushing of the river sounded like a sob.

Chapter 19

Mia

||||||||||||||||||||||||||||||||||||||||||||||||||||||||||||||||||||||||||||||||||||||||||||||||||||||||||||

My dog didn't come back. I never saw him again.

At least the floodwaters receded in the following days, and the river returned to its usual boundaries. Except in the curve where the Stonebrooks' house stood, where for some puzzling reason, the murky water seemed to accumulate. It swept away the fertile topsoil in Iris's vegetable garden and—in spite of the frantic efforts of the family—finally sloshed sluggishly down the basement stairs. Twice they had to have their basement pumped out by the fire department.

The damage was enormous, but the thing that made Iris most bitter was that all her carefully canned foods were spoiled. There was nothing to do but throw them away. For days, Alex, Jay, and their father were busy clearing the downstairs rooms of the heavy sludge the river had left behind. I often helped for a few hours; we pushed wheelbarrow after wheelbarrow filled with dirt outside, and scraped it off the walls.

≈≈≈≈≈

After a while, the horrid smell was so omnipresent I hardly noticed it anymore. But when I stepped into the foyer that one afternoon, the biting stench overpowered me. It smelled like the house itself was on its deathbed, a living thing rotting away.

"Hello, is anybody home?" I called. I thought I heard a voice coming from the kitchen and peered in the doorway. There was no light on, so I thought I had been mistaken. But then I noticed the slumped figure at the table.

It was Iris. With her head propped on her hands, she rocked herself back and forth stiffly. I heard her quietly muttering to herself, but I couldn't understand the words. She seemed to be deeply immersed in studying something that lay in front of her on the scratched surface of the table. I knew I should leave her alone, but I couldn't control my curiosity. Just a quick peek . . .

Cautiously, I crept closer to peer over her shoulder. Now I could understand what she murmured repetitively: it was her daughter's name! She strung the syllables together like the beads of a rosary until they formed a monotonous liturgy: "Oh, Katarina, Katarina . . ."

A floorboard creaked under my weight and her head immediately turned around. For an instant, a strange mixture of fear and joy shone in her eyes. Then she recognized me— and it was extinguished again. "Oh, it's just you," she said dully.

"Yes, it's me. Who were you expecting?"

"Hmmm. For a minute there, dumb old woman that I am, I thought it would be my daughter," Iris said with a sad little smile, running a hand across her face. It occurred to me that it might not have been age that had carved the folds into her skin but deep suffering. It was shocking, even frightening, to see how old and fragile she seemed today and how much I had come to care for her, my "adoptive grandmother."

"Could I maybe make you a cup of tea?" I asked.

"Just sit with me for a minute, Mia. In this house full of men I'm happy for a little female company." Obediently, I pulled up a chair. On the table lay a photograph—so that's what she had been studying so carefully. I recognized the picture; it was the family portrait that had caught my attention the first time I visited the Stonebrooks' house. Katarina's smile was just as mysterious as it had been then.

"You never did tell me how your daughter's story continued . . . why she finally went away," I said, driven by sudden curiosity.

"Right you are," the grandmother murmured. "Well. I did tell you how dissatisfied Katarina was with her life in this small town. There was no way to have a career, or travel to faraway places. At some point, she started to hold Eric responsible for all her broken dreams. She noticeably cut herself off from him, Katarina did, and spent more and more time with the children. They built that tree house over there on the island together. They created their own little world, and no one else could get in. Not even Eric." With her index finger, Iris bored holes in the air in the kitchen. "Such craziness! Instead of taking care of her household, like a decent woman should. Often there wasn't so much as a crust of bread in the house when I came to visit!" the old woman said with indignation. "I asked what she did with the money for the groceries and such. And my daughter ran off to proudly present some new lens for her camera. It didn't take long before the neighbors started talking, saying that Katarina let her children run wild, that she wandered up and down the river with them and only did as she pleased—without paying any heed at all to her husband! She was a walking scandal, our Katarina!" Shaking her head, Iris looked down at her folded hands. As if praying would have been any use.

"Of course Eric heard the rumors, too. In the bar, the men gave him a hard time about not having his 'wild woman' under control and did he need help taming her? It wasn't long before everyone in town had decided that the young lady was leading him by the nose—and that Eric was blinded by love and let it happen. It was clear who wore the pants in the Stonebrook household. Katarina made him a laughingstock. It must have been hard for a man as proud as Eric."

I looked at the family photograph. Until now, Eric had always been something of a side note to Katarina's story. But now I asked myself how he must have felt about all of this.

"The most painful part of it for him was probably that there was a bit of truth in the mockery," Iris continued. "You have to know that Eric has always idolized his wife. It's a terrible thing when one person loves more than the other, my dear. Because the one who loves more is always weaker, more easily hurt. Eric knew that. 'I should have let her go back then,' he once told me later, when everything was long over. 'I should have let her go, but I couldn't. Katarina was my life.' Eric was distraught. He forbade her to swim naked in the river. But of course she did it anyway," Iris added with a snort. "She did it more than ever! That's how she was, our Katarina. The more Eric tried to hold on to her, the more fiercely she struggled against him. But all he wanted was for her to stay home and take care of her responsibilities, just like everyone else."

She shrugged her shoulders in a small, resigned gesture. It was clear that she had never understood her daughter. But I wanted to understand this. Spellbound, I hung on the older woman's every word, entirely wrapped up in Katarina's story.

"Because their financial situation wasn't exactly rosy, Eric started to check how Katarina was spending their money . . . and then there was no more expensive camera equipment. From then on, Katarina was supposed to keep records and account for what she spent. They had some terrible fights because of it. Their battles raged through the house and shook the walls." A chill ran through her at the memory of it. "Katarina was a fearsome opponent! A terrible hothead. When she was in a rage, she fought with any means. She even threw dishes!

"The poor boys were completely upset, and I often took them to my house. Oh, I tried to talk some sense into Katarina. But it was pointless, absolutely pointless! It only made her more bitter. Sometimes, she didn't even let me into the house. 'I'm grounded,' she said through the screen with no expression on her face. And once she had a black eye."

"What? You mean Eric actually . . . he *hit* her?" I cried with shock. What an idiot to treat his wife that way. No wonder she ran away from him.

"I don't know if that's really true," Iris replied. Her arthritic fingers reached for my hand to soothe me. "You never met her, but Katarina always knew how to make things appear the way she wanted them to . . ."

I freed my hand from her grasp. "That sounds as if you were on Eric's side. I don't understand. Katarina is your daughter! Why didn't you help her?" My words sounded harsher than I had intended. Like an accusation. Iris sank her gaze.

"Well, my husband and I didn't want to interfere," she explained, more to the kitchen table and the family photo than to me. "We thought we had raised her too leniently, spoiled her too much—she was our only child, after all. We thought it was our fault that she had turned out so wild, so headstrong." She touched the cold glass covering the photograph thoughtfully, as if she wanted to stroke her daughter's face. Her stern features softened. "Maybe you're right, dear. Maybe we were too hard on her. She was still so young, our Katarina."

I couldn't bear to say another harsh word in reply. I felt sorry for her, the way she sat there, bent like an old tree growing on cliffs with its roots clinging to the sparse dirt. No matter how much Iris still clung to her infallible righteousness, she had long sensed that this was only *her* truth. She could recite the Hail Mary into eternity, but it wouldn't undo the mistakes she had made.

Maybe that was why she had told me Katarina's story, to receive some kind of absolution. But I couldn't give it to her. We both knew that.

Looking lost, Iris continued her story. "When I came to visit, I often found Katarina at the river. She always loved to be down by the water. 'The river is my heart,' she would often say with a laugh. But that day she didn't laugh as she stared into the stream. 'Do you know where the water goes, Mom?' she asked me quietly, throwing sticks in the water to be carried away by the current. That penetrating tone in her voice. But I didn't have an answer for her. So she answered herself: 'Away, just away from here. . . . If it weren't for the boys . . .' She didn't end the sentence, and I didn't ask her to. That was the last time I spoke with my daughter. A few days later, I moved in with them—my husband had already died by then. And you know the rest of the story."

I nodded glumly and didn't want to see the family photo anymore. Because now I knew that it was only an illusion of happy days that they had never had. This time I let Iris pat my hand. "I'm afraid when I have such an attentive listener I just babble on and on," she sighed, and it sounded as if she almost regretted having told me so much. "Don't worry your pretty head about an old woman's talk! That's all ancient history."

Oh, how wrong she was!

But she meant well when she added, "Now go! The boys finished their work in the basement earlier. Alexander wanted to take a shower. I'm sure he's already waiting for you." So I stood up and left her alone with the faded picture of her daughter.

Before I left, I saw her dry lips start to form words again: answers that it was too late for now. I saw the mother call the beloved name without a sound, knowing she would never receive an answer. Then I closed the kitchen door behind me.

~~~~~

After that talk, and the feel of the elderly woman's wrinkled hand on mine, it was good to be with Alex, who felt warm and alive.

He had just gotten out of the shower, and his curly hair was still dark with wet. Now he lay resting next to me on the bed, naked and entirely unself-conscious. I, however, still wore my underwear. In the beginning, Alex had had to woo me with a thousand sweet words every time he slipped the clothes off my body. That wasn't the case anymore, but I was still always on my guard when we were together.

At that moment, though, as I lay in Alex's arms and felt his calm breathing, I felt at peace. Even though it certainly was odd to know so much about his vanished mother . . . maybe even more than Alex himself. I would have liked to talk to him about it, but we had an unspoken agreement that the subject of Katarina—as well as questions about my ex-boyfriend—were strictly off limits between us. His grandmother was right, all of that belonged to the distant past.

I was here with Alex in the present, and that's all that mattered.

Lazily, I stretched out my arm and nudged the globe standing on the nightstand. Its warm light wandered over the walls and bathed our faces in a sea-blue and ochre-yellow glow. Our little world ... I turned the globe again and let my fingers glide across the continents.

"Where would you most like to go, Alex?" I asked. I loved to laze around talking with him about curious and silly things. "Come on, what's your dream destination?"

Alex grumbled, "Anywhere there's no muck that needs to be hauled out of the basement! My dream destination is where you are." He blew in my ear and whispered, "I love you, Mia. And I want to sleep with you." Playfully, he tugged at the strap of my bra.

It was as if someone had poured a bucket of ice-cold water over me. How was it possible that those few words could simultaneously plunge me into a state of rapture and panic? *Heart-pounding, stomach-wrenching, limb-freezing panic.*

For in that moment it became clear to me how close, how dangerously close, Alex had gotten to me. How ridiculous my halfhearted attempts to keep him at a distance had been. Just like my refusal to play the cello for him, even though all my inner soundscapes leaned toward him ...

For a heartbeat, I longed to just give in to that gravity, to let myself fall. To tell Alex everything.

But that would mean throwing my painstakingly repaired glass heart at him and trusting that he would catch it. No, I couldn't take the risk! If I did, I'd be defenseless, utterly exposed.

And I already felt so naked! There was only my thin skin as a protective wall. And when Alex touched me, like now, it was as if his fingers could sink deep into my innermost self. I was like hot wax under those hands. Pliable, without a shape, with no will of my own.

How could I have let things get so far again? Hadn't I learned anything from the disaster with Nicolas? How could I ever get out of this situation unharmed? I was caught in a trap. Chaos reigned in my head, everything swayed. But maybe that was just me.

Driftwood.

"What is it, Mia? Are you okay?" Alex asked anxiously.

I sat up straight. I had sworn to myself that I'd never be driftwood again. *Never again!*

And suddenly those mean words came to me. Honed to a sharp edge, they lay on the tip of my tongue. All I had to do was open my mouth, and they shot out: "I kissed Jay, out on the island."

I saw how the words slowly sank into his consciousness, like stones thrown into deep water. "What?" Alex asked, as if he hadn't quite understood. As if he wanted to give me a chance to say "Just kidding!" or "Oh, nothing. You must have misunderstood."

But I didn't do him the favor. Mercilessly, I repeated the sentence, hammered the words into his very being: "*I kissed your brother!*" This time he got the message. I could see it. Something broke.

"You did what? Why . . . why did you do that?" he stammered. His face was white as chalk. I had just thrown his world out of alignment. Our world.

Continents drifted apart, were abandoned. Islands were swallowed up by cold ocean waters.

And it was me that had caused it! ME! With just a few words. It was strange that I seemed to possess such power over another person. He was the one who loved more. His weakness gave me strength. His falling apart gave me form.

For just a brief moment, a feeling of triumph I had never known before coursed through me. It was as if I had done it for Katarina, too. As if I had shown everyone who thought they could treat their women like driftwood, all the idiots like Nicolas and Eric.

But then I realized with painful clarity that it was Alex who sat there next to me on the bed. My boyfriend, who had trusted me. Who had just told me that he loved me.

He wrapped his arms around himself as if he had just realized that he was naked. As if he wanted to cover his bareness. Then I had to turn my gaze away. I jumped up from the bed and turned on the normal light. The magical glow of our globe was extinguished in the relentless brightness of the overhead light, which burned my eyes. Hectically, I started to gather my strewn-about clothes.

"What's going on between you and Jay?" Alex asked very quietly behind me. Then louder. "Talk to me, Mia! Please!"

That was the first time he had asked me for something. But I didn't answer. I couldn't.

With one leg in my jeans, I hopped to the door. Get away, I just had to get away from here! I couldn't bear it one second longer!

I left. I left him. I had betrayed him.

Alex didn't stop me.

Even on my way home, I didn't cry. I looked up into the sad, lifeless branches of my cherry tree. It was hard to believe that we had sat there together just last summer, between the swaying fruits. Exchanging kisses. That must have been a thousand years ago.

My heart isn't a stone, I had warned Alex back then. But now it felt just like one, as if I had nothing but a dry cherry pit in my chest that was so hard it hurt to breathe.

Third Intermezzo

||||||||||||||||||||||||||||||||||||||||||||||||||||||||||||||||||||||||||||||||||||||||||||||||||||||||||||||||

I'm not alone in the hole in the ice anymore. Right next to me the water is bubbling as if something is rising, slowly surfacing, out of the depths of the river.

It's a woman. Her long, light hair floats on the water. Her skin is whiter than the ice. The eyes are like dark holes in her pale face.

Where did she come from? Did she come to help me? I feel like I should know her somehow . . .

What's a dream, and what's real?

I blink woozily. It's getting harder and harder to think clearly. But one thing I still know: something is wrong here. The woman can't possibly be here! I don't understand what's going on, but you can't see her breath in the icy air—there's no breath to be seen!

I want to pull away, but then she's touching my cheek. Her hand is as cold as death . . . no . . . all the cold softens. It's warm . . . as warm as summer! I feel safe and laugh with joy because now I finally recognize her again!

"You . . . you!" I whisper.

"Yes, me. I came to get you."

To get me . . .

Braids of hair wind themselves toward me like pale tentacles, coiling themselves around my arms. But I only have eyes for her smile. Ice crystals glitter on her eyelids. How terribly I've missed her!

"Come. Come with me! We'll live deep in the river and reign over the fish. We'll be the lords of the kingfishers! Come where there's no sadness and no pain. No lonesomeness, never again. I promise you," she whispered. "We'll be together forever."

I . . . I'm not sure. It's like when you've dived so deep that you don't know which way is up and which way is down. I hesitate . . . look at my numb hands, which are still grasping the edge of the ice.

"Let go! What's still holding you here in this sad place? Come with me into the river."

Yes, you're right. Nothing and no one keep me here . . . want to follow you, your smile . . . anywhere.

But wait. What's that? My name . . . is someone calling my name?

L'INVERNO
WINTER

Chapter 20

Alexander

~~~~~~

I couldn't understand it. I just didn't get it! I had just told Mia that I love her, that I want her. And POW!

It was as if I had jumped off the high dive, but instead of being enveloped in warm water, I had crashed into concrete.

I kissed your brother. . . . Her words echoed endlessly in my brain. And my fantasy provided the fitting images for the scene—Mia and Jay, kissing each other passionately, and not only that. She had probably only played the prude with me, while with him . . . damn it!

My thoughts were tied in knots, none of it made any sense. Why had Mia even told me this in the first place?

I kissed your brother . . . kissed your brother . . . pounded through my brain painfully, again and again, until it felt like my head had swollen to the size of a watermelon. What I really wanted to do was ram my head against a wall so it would finally stop.

That night, I barely closed my eyes, tossing and turning in my knotted sheets.

When I woke up from my restless slumber the next day, for a fleeting moment I thought I had only dreamed the whole mess. My girlfriend couldn't possibly have cheated on me with my little brother! That couldn't really have happened.

But apparently, it could. After all, Mia herself had confessed to me! With an angry cry, I hurled my pillow against the wall. I felt the rage pumping through my veins—red and hot and powerful. The confusion and pain of yesterday evening, everything was carried away by a tremendous surge of rage. It felt good not to feel anything else.

I gritted my teeth. How dare the two of them—right in front of my eyes, and yet behind my back! Scenes from the previous months came to mind. Now, suddenly, I saw through everything with crystal clear, razor-sharp clarity. How could I have been so blind not to notice what was going on between them?

Jay's blushing when Mia came to visit us. The stolen glances they exchanged, as if they shared a secret, as if there was something special between them. Yes, I had been a trusting idiot, but the two of them were . . .

"Traitors!" I whispered.

At that moment, my grandmother came through the door. "What are you still doing here, Alexander?" she scolded, without noticing my dark expression. "Did you oversleep? It's almost nine o'clock already! Come on, rise and shine. School started a long time ago!"

There was no point in arguing with Grandma. Besides, I didn't want those two traitors to think I would crawl away from them to lick my wounds like a dog that's been kicked. I got up to get dressed.

I arrived at school with my head held high. The break must have just started. My friends stood in their usual corner of the schoolyard.

"Hey, Alex, you sleepyhead!" Wolf called cheerfully, waving to me. I ignored him and glanced around the courtyard, looking for them.

Mia stood over there, my ex-ex-ex-girlfriend. I stared her right in the face, my anger engulfing me like a pulsing protective shield. Even if she messed around with Jay right in front of me, it wouldn't have mattered to me anymore. I was done with her.

I tried to tell her all that with my look, pouring my entire burning disdain into it. Apparently, Mia got it, because she looked at the ground with shame. Her face looked pale and miserable. It served her right! If she even had a conscience, she was discovering it awfully late! I did wonder, though, why her lover wasn't with her. Who was this farce supposed to fool now?

I spied Jay over by the garbage cans, where he was recording the crackling of discarded aluminum foil with his tape recorder. With a heavy plop, a half-eaten apple landed in the bin. The shrimp, who had thrown away the apple, tapped his forehead behind Jay's back to indicate he was crazy. "What a dimwit!"

Normally, I would have given the midget a pounding for that. Normally.

Still boiling with rage, I stepped up to Jay. He turned to me with a smile. "Morning, Skip!" When he saw my expression, he furrowed his brow questioningly. "What's wrong?"

My traitorous brother. Still playing the innocent one.

"Do you have a thing for Mia?" I asked abruptly. Jay seemed surprised that I knew about it but nodded without hesitating. I balled my hands into fists in the pockets of my jacket, and then relaxed them again. Between clenched teeth I spat, "Mia said you two kissed each other." I wanted him to explain what he'd done! I wanted to hear it from his mouth!

"Yeah. We kissed each other," Jay replied calmly.

My whole life, my grandmother had hammered into me that I should look out for my little brother. And damn it, I'd done it! I had helped him with his homework. I'd towed the annoying nuisance around when my friends and I got together. I'd even gotten into fights for this idiot when people made fun of him!

Jay had never thanked me for anything. And I hadn't expected him to. The only thing I had expected from him was loyalty. We'd even sworn it with a blood oath!

But how did this rat of a brother thank me for busting my butt for him for years and years? He stole my girlfriend, the only thing that was important to me!

And now, Jay even had the audacity to just say that to my face! Without the slightest trace of regret!

I think that's what finally pushed me over the edge. "You . . . you goddamned punk!" I hissed and tore into him.

I couldn't remember ever hitting my brother. He was a slacker as an opponent—didn't really even defend himself.

"Fight, there's a fight!" someone yelled in the background. Out of the corner of my eye, I saw several onlookers crowd around us and noted Mia's horrified face among them.

I threw a solid hit to Jay's nose, which immediately began to bleed. The blood made bizarre patterns on his face. I observed it with grim satisfaction.

Jay didn't cry. Then I would have stopped. On his face was more an expression of bewilderment, as if I was treating him unfairly. But I was the one who had been betrayed here.

Filled with rage, I began to shake him. "How long has this been going on between you and Mia? How long have you been playing this game behind my back?" I hissed into his ear. I shook him as if I wanted to rattle the truth loose. His head bobbed back and forth helplessly. He didn't have a chance to answer me.

The guys pulled me away from him. "Calm down, man! Have you totally lost your mind, or what?" Matt cried, staring at me. "He's your brother!"

"He WAS!" I spat in Jay's direction. "Get out of my sight."

Jay looked like he wanted to say something, but then he just shook his head and trotted away.

Lunchtime passed in icy silence that day. "Can you please give me the salt?" I asked Grandma, even though the saltshaker was directly in front of Jay. She gave it to me, all the time scolding both of us with steely blue eyes as if we were two felons.

I asked myself if someone from school had called home because of the fight. And sure enough, a short while later Dad asked—while looking straight at me—"What happened to your nose, Jay?"

Jay wriggled uncomfortably on his chair and mumbled, "I banged into something . . . bloody nose . . . stupid clumsiness."

"Ah. I heard you got into a fistfight with your brother," our father countered, glaring at us both sternly.

"My grandsons, two uncivilized ruffians! What a scandal!" Grandma wailed. "What is the world coming to, that I have to experience this!" With that, she withdrew to the kitchen sink and started rattling pots and pans.

Apart from that, it was very quiet. Jay and I pushed around the food on our plates, which was cold by now. "I'm not hungry," my brother finally murmured and fled from the room.

Just as I was about to make my escape, too, my father said sharply, "You stay put!" Against my will, I sat back down across from him at the other end of the table.

If I had only felt better after beating up Jay. But unfortunately, it hadn't done any good, and now I was going to get a serious talking to as well.

"What were you fighting about, you and Jay?" Dad grumbled, restlessly twirling the tassels of the tablecloth between his thick fingers. "What on earth has gotten into you boys? You've always been a team!"

I shrugged my shoulders defiantly and stared at my fingers, which had also begun picking at the tablecloth. I had powerful hands with odd, square fingernails. My father's hands. With a sudden start, I realized that I was much more like him than I had ever wanted to acknowledge.

I had never paid attention before, but when I looked up, I saw my straight, narrow nose on his face. My thick eyebrows. The way he ran his fingers through his graying curls, just like I did when I was at a loss for something to say.

It was creepy, as if I were looking into a distorted mirror that made me look years older. That's exactly how I would look at forty: abandoned by the woman I loved. Trapped in a job I didn't like, I'd still be sitting tight in this miserable town. By then I would have forgotten that I once had other dreams . . .

My father sighed; he probably thought I was keeping silent out of sheer stubbornness. "I have to get back to work, Alexander. The lunch break is almost over. We'll talk later." He stood up and moved toward the door. I watched as he wiped his clean shoes on the doormat out of habit and felt an extraordinary exhaustion overcome me.

~~~~~

The weeks passed, but the feeling of exhaustion had a tight grip on me. I went to school, did things with my buddies, and helped Grandma at home. But there seemed to be a dull film lying over everything.

"You look so pale and tired, Alexander," Grandma said, patting my hand to express her concern. "You should get to bed earlier. And eat more apples. That will keep you healthy!"

When I didn't say anything, Grandma leaned forward confidentially. "It's because of Mia, isn't it? I don't know what happened between you, but she's a good person. Maybe you two should talk to each other again? And by the Holy Mother of God," she suddenly started scolding, "find a way to get along with your brother again! After all, it's almost Christmas!"

Christmas or not, I couldn't bring myself to forgive Jay. For Grandma's sake, we at least kept a tense truce. At the table, I asked Jay for the salt, and he passed it to me. But we limited ourselves to talking with each other only when absolutely necessary. Otherwise, we kept out of each other's way.

I hadn't spoken to Mia since she made her confession. At least the lovebirds were discreet, so I never had to deal with the sight of them standing around making out at school.

~~~~~

Christmas, the festival of love and reconciliation, somehow came and went. What didn't come, again, was a message from my mother. And I really could have used some sign of life from her right then. Using the globe and the old photographs, I tried to travel to her in my thoughts, but it didn't work anymore. No matter how long I pressed her shell to my ear, instead of hearing the sound of the ocean, now I only heard the monotone thudding of my own pulse in my ears.

Through the pictures she had sent me over the years, I had at least had the feeling that my mother was still a part of my life—that we were still connected to each other in spite of the distance between us. Only now did I admit that I had lost her forever. Mama wasn't just on a long, long trip. The truth was that she had abandoned and betrayed me, just like Mia and Jay had done.

Apparently, it didn't mean anything to Katarina to be my mother. Otherwise, she would have come to get me. She would have visited me. She would have at least kept sending me pictures from all her travels. She wouldn't have left me in the first place. My mother might as well have been dead.

Maybe that would have been easier.

I decided to be done with her, once and for all. So I put my globe marked with all Katarina's destinations and the boxes with all the photos she had sent me in the next garbage collection.

I tried to feel a sense of satisfaction that I had finally buried that stupid, little boy fantasy. But when I looked out the window and saw the globe perched on a pile of garbage in the rain, all I felt was empty.

I started taking long walks along the river. A thin sheet of ice had already started to form along the shore. I drew the fresh air into my lungs and hoped it would chase away the nasty thoughts that circled around me like vultures, boring their pointed beaks into my soft innards.

My mother and my girlfriend both left me. My brother betrayed me. Maybe there was something wrong with me? Was I impossible to get along with? I pondered these things as the frozen grass splintered under my feet.

In spite of the cold spell toward the end of the month, it had snowed only sparingly. The white powder lay like a shabby, threadbare cloth over the frozen world. There was no one else to be seen far and wide, not someone walking a dog, or even a bird. It seemed like I was the last living creature on the planet. Utterly alone, lost somehow under the weight of the empty sky.

The clouds hung so low that the sky and the earth merged. I couldn't recognize any horizon. Everything was gray.

I had the feeling this gray would eventually suffocate me. From all sides it pressed on me, as my world continued to shrink, reduced to the size of the discarded globe. It was as though there were nothing left of my life anymore, nothing left of Skip.

No, I would never leave this place. I knew that now.

I would die without ever seeing the ocean.

Chapter 21

Jay

||||||||||||||||||||||||||||||||||||||||||||||||||||||||||||||||||||||||||||||||||||||||||||||||||||||||||||||||||||||||||||||

The hiss of the blades cut through the winter stillness. I didn't need to look over at the river to know that it was Skip. Even though it was beginning to slowly thaw again, he went ice-skating every day. For hours, he drew circles on the ice, a lonely skater on the gray-white band of the river.

With a sigh, I picked up my shopping bag again and kept walking. My route home led me past Mia's house. Her cello was silent. Only the cherry tree hummed softly, sunken in silver-blue winter dreams. Behind its bare branches, I could make out a pale oval—Mia's face.

Recently, I had often seen her sitting up there at her window and how she looked over toward our house. Just like she had done earlier, before she started coming over to visit us. I think she missed us. Not just Skip, but Grandma, too. Maybe even me.

When Mia noticed that I was staring up at her, she raised her arm to wave to me—but then immediately let her hand fall again.

I had no idea why she had told Skip about our kiss. After all, that was strictly between her and me and didn't have anything to do with my brother. Although he certainly thought it did.

For a while, I had been mad at Mia for that. At Skip, too. The dumb lug was more interested in swinging his fists than listening to me! His loss . . . that way I couldn't explain it to him, and he had to go on being miserable.

The whole situation was so stupid! Back when we were all together, everything had been fine. Now all of us were alone. Skip. Jay.

Mia.

I looked up at her. She looked so sad. She was probably suffering from the same sickness I was: loneliness.

I waved to Mia and her face lit up. A moment later, she came running out of the house, without a hat or a scarf. As she drew closer, her steps slowed down. A few steps away from me, Mia stopped and scraped patterns in the snow with her boot. She didn't dare to look straight at me.

"How's your nose, Jay?" she finally asked.

I patted my face. "Everything's still attached, see? I think it hurt Skip more than me."

"So, how's he doing?" It was supposed to sound casual, but her voice was raw and sore.

"No idea, he doesn't talk to me. But I don't think he's doing very well." We both looked over to the river. Skip was a good skater, but today he was sprinting like he was

197

possessed. He drew his circles tighter and tighter, faster and faster. I could hear how his thoughts were churning in circles, endlessly, uselessly, spinning around like a dog chasing its tail.

Mia sighed. "I'm so sorry about all of this. I got you involved in it, Jay. I used you . . . used you as a way to hurt Alex." She fiddled with the little cross on a silver chain that my brother had given her. "I should have trusted Alex, should have told him what was going on with me. But I was too scared. Can you understand that?" she whispered so quietly I could hardly hear her. "I . . . I ruined everything." Mia covered her face with her hands like she wanted to hide behind them. "It's my fault that everyone's unhappy now! I broke our blood oath!"

Gently, I pulled her hands away from her face. "It probably wasn't in keeping with the blood oath to kiss my brother's girlfriend, was it?" I asked.

The corners of Mia's mouth curled into a weak smile. "Probably not."

"So then I would be just as guilty as you. Guilt is a stupid word, anyway. I don't believe in it. Some things we just have to do, because we can't help it. Even if they're wrong. At that moment, you know, I just had to kiss you, otherwise I would have exploded!"

Mia smiled, but then became serious again when I said, "Maybe some promises just can't be kept. Because things change. And all of us change, too. I always had to promise Alina something, too . . ."

"Like what?"

"That I would never forget her. And only have eyes for her. She wanted me to have nothing but Alina in my head, nothing and no one else. But I sometimes wanted to try out new things. Vivaldi's music. Kissing a girl. I knew for sure that Alina would be mad at me if I did."

"But you did it anyway!"

"Yup. I broke my promise, and everything is different now." I hadn't ever admitted that, not even to myself, but now I said it. "I miss Alina. Everything here reminds me of her. The river. She always said, 'The river is my heart.'"

"The river is my heart?" Mia repeated, looking at me with a confused expression. "I've heard that before! Your grandmother told me that . . ." She interrupted herself. I could hear how her thoughts were racing in her head. She rewound her memories to examine certain things again. Just like my recordings. Sometimes the individual sounds suddenly made sense, formed a melody.

"Who is Alina? How did you meet her?" she asked, her voice trembling a little.

I could see that Mia was freezing. "Alina was always there, ever since I can remember," I said. "Her real name is Katarina, but when I was little, I couldn't say the 'r' and called her Katalina. Later that got shortened to Alina. It was my nickname for her."

She looked so strange. She blinked several times, as if she weren't entirely awake. "Wait a minute . . ." she said as if in slow motion. "Do you mean to tell me that Katarina and Alina are the same . . ."

But she didn't finish her sentence, because in that moment we both noticed it: the scraping of Skip's ice skates had stopped! Instead, there was a silence buzzing in my ears.

I looked over toward the river. Skip had disappeared, as if the earth had swallowed him. *Or the river . . .*

"Alina!" I whispered.

Already, I knew something terrible had happened. She couldn't get me, I was careful. But Skip . . . he didn't have anything that could protect him anymore. Not even his silver cross necklace. Mia was wearing it now.

"What's wrong, Jay?" I heard Mia call. It sounded more like a sob. But I had already dropped the shopping bag and started running toward the river's edge. I had covered about half the distance when I heard his cries: "Help! Help! I fell through the ice!"

No doubt about it. That was Skip! I tried to run faster, but every step, every breath, seemed like an eternity.

"Help, why doesn't anyone help me?"

I'm coming! I wanted to cry, but the words were strangled before they reached my lips. My panting breath caught painfully in my chest.

There, finally! Before me stretched the milk-white curves of the river. I plunged down through the bushes, past the willows that looked like long-haired witches with their hanging branches.

When I stepped on the ice, it whispered words I couldn't understand. I forced myself to make slow, careful movements, as if I were approaching a wild animal, wanting to gain its trust. I caressed it with my feet, even though every fiber of my being urged me to hurry, go faster, fast, fast, before it was too late.

The farther I felt my way out onto the winter river, the more horrible it got. Cracks spread out under my feet along the frozen surface of the skin. Their creaking and crackling sounded like tearing silk: d-jang! d-jang! I flinched like a whip was cracking on my back.

The cracks in the ice reminded me of a giant spiderweb—and I was stuck right in the middle of it. Far out on the river. Unsure of myself, I looked over at the shore. It was Mia! She was running toward our house. She must be getting help! I wasn't alone after all and that gave me courage. And I surely needed it.

The ice below me was black, a lurking abyss. Its words were clearly understandable now. It whined under my every step, moaning terrible threats: *Go back, go back,* it creaked. *I'll be the death of you!*

But I didn't turn back. "I'm n-not scared," I sang to the river in reply. "No, I'm not afraid of you!" That was a lie. But you don't have to be truly scared until it suddenly goes silent. That's the moment when the river tears open its hungry old jaws to swallow you up . . . just like it wanted to swallow my brother.

To keep that from happening to me, too, I got down on all fours to distribute my weight better. The last few yards I scooted on my stomach. Just a little bit closer—then I was finally there!

The gaping wound in the ice was directly in front of me. Its jagged edges looked like broken teeth. I saw blood. And trapped in the hole, my brother! I called his name: "Skip, Skip!"

"Jay?" he whispered in disbelief, like someone who's not sure if he's still dreaming.

"Yes, I'm here. Give me your hand!" With an enormous effort, he stretched out his right arm, and I grabbed his hand. It was cut up badly. I felt his blood, slippery on my fingers. "Good, now the other one!"

But Skip's left hand fell limply back into the water. "Can't anymore . . . Jay!" he gasped. He had fought with the icy river, but now he was tired.

"Try it again, Skip!" I urged him. But already he wasn't listening to me. Instead, his head was tilted as if he was listening to another voice, one that came out of the water.

"Do you hear that . . . she's calling me . . . she wants me to come with her," he whispered with an odd smile. "Our mother! She's down there, Jay!"

I shuddered. "Don't listen! You have to concentrate on me!" Skip didn't answer. He was already far off and floated further and further away.

But I felt a new level of terror when I saw his eyes: the irises had turned a green-brown color, as if the river were already flowing through them. I could feel his grasp loosening.

"Don't let go of my hand! Don't you *dare* let go of my hand! You are not going to die on me out here, or. . . . Don't let go, Skip, please!" I screamed at him, I cursed at him, I begged him to stay here with me. "Come on, Skip! Think of all the trips you're still going to take, and everything else you'll miss out on!" It was no use. I cried in desperation because he didn't want to let me help him.

"Please, Skip! We need you more than she does!" I sobbed, and finally my words got through to him. The blue in my brother's eyes was almost extinguished already. There was only a tiny spark of Skip left.

But that spark somehow helped him grasp my hand. Skip's weight pulled me forward, toward the hole. The winter river was greedy. It didn't want to release my brother. And it wanted to have me, too.

Skip moaned as he was torn in two. It was as if something—someone—were attached to his legs like a lead weight, trying to pull us underwater.

With gritted teeth, I planted my feet in the ice and resisted. My shoulders felt like they were being pulled out of their sockets. And still, I continued to slide relentlessly toward the edge of the ice . . . toward our death.

My arms were already dipping into the water. Deathly cold reached for me, climbed farther up my body on its way to my heart.

Suddenly, a tremendous rage overtook me, flowing hot through my veins. "No, Alina, you aren't getting him!" I bellowed. "Not Skip, and not me, either! We belong to the living, do you hear me!"

There was a white form under the ice. It could have been a dead fish or a plastic bag . . . or a face pressed against the ice from below! With my last ounce of energy, I screamed at it: "This is *our* life, Alina! You won't steal it from us!"

I don't know how we did it. Maybe she finally did let go, let us go. I only know that somehow we were back on firm ice. We lay there motionless, completely drained and exhausted, holding each other.

We were safe now, but I was afraid Skip might still die. He was entirely white, and so cold, in spite of my efforts to warm him.

But then I saw his eyes slowly gain back their blue, the blue of the ocean, and then I knew that Alina had lost.

Chapter 22

Mia

||||||||||||||||||||||||||||||||||||||||||||||||||||||||||||||||||||||||||||||||||||||||||||||||||||||||||||||||||||

Wednesday, January 22, nighttime

Dear Alex,

I've heard that you're doing better now. You sure gave us a scare! Jay, your father, your grandma—and me.

But I'm not writing you because you almost drowned. I'm writing because I have to explain a few things to you. I should have done it a long time ago. It's so hard to find the right words! This is my fifth try. The others all landed in the garbage can. This time, though, I'm going to just keep on writing and put the letter in your mailbox tomorrow. This time I won't wimp out again!

You should finally know the truth, my truth.

Everything started a year and a half ago, when my parents decided to move here. I was so mad at them. They treated me like a dumb little kid that didn't have a say in anything, even though I was already fifteen!

That was around the time I met Nicolas. I hung out with the smokers at school, and he asked me if I had a light. I did.

Nicolas was three years ahead of me in school and had his own car. How unbelievably cool and grown up he seemed!

"That boy is too old for you, Mia!" my parents protested. But what did they know? I couldn't explain to them that my friends envied me because I was going out with such a cool guy. I couldn't tell them how fantastic I felt when he looked at me with this desire in his eyes that was completely new to me and made my skin tingle.

The more my mother complained, the more appealing it was for me to meet with Nicolas secretly. Finally, there was a chance to invite him over to my house. My parents were visiting some friends that night. The minute the door closed behind them, I put a bottle of wine in the fridge to chill. I had prepared everything, even bought him flowers, yellow roses that I put in a crystal vase. They filled the living room with an inviting fragrance. I scattered a few rose petals over the sofa. They felt like silk on my skin.

I wanted ... actually, I have no idea what I wanted. Probably everything you see in the movies: love, closeness, happiness. Everything larger than life. Maybe I just wanted someone to finally recognize me, to see in me the woman I wanted to become. Beautiful, confident, grown up. The woman my parents refused to see. Pretty naïve, isn't it?

After Nicolas arrived, we sat on the sofa in the living room. "Nice place you have here," he said, checking out my parents' antiques. Because I was so nervous and didn't really know what should happen next, I drank a glass of wine. And then another one.

We made out for a while, and then I finally got up the nerve to ask him if I should play something on the cello for him.

I played my favorite piece for him, the largo from Vivaldi's "Winter" concerto, that sounds so much like thawing snow. While I plucked the strings, I hoped Nicolas could hear my true self resonating in the notes.

After just a few measures, I already felt his hand on my knee. "Nice," he said, and started kissing me again. And then somehow we were lying on the sofa. Nicolas pushed himself on me and suddenly had his hands everywhere. Under my T-shirt. Under my skirt. Between my legs.

It all went so fast, I hardly knew what was happening. Halfheartedly, I tried to push Nicolas away. He asked me why I was so skittish. "You want it, too," he said and just kept on going—ignored me saying no.

I was so upset and disoriented, and my head was spinning from the wine. Was Nicolas right? Hadn't I provoked him? At some point, I gave up and just let things happen to me.

When Nicolas was finally finished, he stood up to get dressed. "Where are you going?" I asked, confused.

"Leaving. I'm out of here," he said as he pulled up his jeans. He bumped into my cello, which was leaning against the coffee table. It crashed to the ground with a dissonant clatter. I heard one of the tuning pegs splinter and break. "Piece of crap!" Nicolas spat, pushing it with his foot.

The sound of the broken strings resonated through the room like the moaning of a wounded animal. I started to cry. Nicolas looked at me, irritated. "What are you crying about now? This stupid wooden box? I'll give you the money to fix it." Then he left, just walked out the door, leaving me behind with my broken cello.

207

After Nicolas had finally gone, I started mechanically gathering the rose petals from the sofa. I put the bouquet in the garbage can, and the crystal vase back in its cabinet. The greasy fingerprints on the glass were easy to wipe away. As if they had never existed.

I had to throw up. Then I took a shower. A petal was still stuck to my left thigh. It was wilted and had brown spots. I turned the shower on harder, and then it was gone. I let the water beat down on me for a long time. It mixed with my tears. It was as if I were being washed away.

Like a piece of driftwood.

I've never talked about this with anyone. Not with my parents, not with my girlfriends. And not with you.

In part, it was my fault what happened to me. Yeah, I got mixed up with the wrong guy. But that happens to other girls, too. Why did this crap throw me so completely for a loop? It was as if I had somehow lost my grip.

At first, I tried to just go on like I had been before. But pretty soon I figured out that wouldn't work. Something had changed, something deep inside me. When I looked in the mirror, I was astonished that I still looked just like I always had. As if nothing at all had happened.

But I wanted it to be visible! I had seen through the adult world now: a world filled with nothing but glittering illusions but no love. There was just sex—people using each other and then throwing them away again. I withdrew as if I were in mourning. I didn't let anyone get near me anymore.

But then you came along, Alex.

You didn't let anything scare you off. Somehow you managed to sneak into my heart. For a long time, I tried to convince myself that it was nothing serious between us, that I had everything under control.

But when you said you wanted to sleep with me, that's when I noticed I had been fooling myself. I got just plain scared. That's why I threw that line at you: "I kissed your brother."

That wasn't a lie. But it was only a fragment of the truth, one I knew would distort the whole picture like a shard of a broken mirror.

Yes, Jay and I kissed each other. A single time . . . no idea why, it just happened. I don't want anything from Jay. He's just a good friend to me. Unfortunately, I repaid him in a rotten way. I used your little brother to get to you. And all of it just to protect myself—I sacrificed both of you for that. Sacrificed you.

And I had sworn to you with a blood oath that I wouldn't leave you.

I did it anyway . . . and the worst part of it is that I left you alone without a single word of explanation! Like your mother. Just like that.

Yes, I knew that would get to you more than everything else. That's exactly why I did it. So much for trust and being there for each other. With that, I went against every aspect of our blood oath. I betrayed everyone. You, Jay. And myself.

I've come to understand that in the past few weeks, while I sat in my room and watched the shadow of my cherry tree as it slowly wandered across the white walls. The cool, clear white used to soothe me—purity, protection. No photos. No memories.

Now, when I try to stare holes into the whiteness, all I see is cold and emptiness. I cheated myself out of us. Out of everything that grew in me last year and everything that might still have been.

I screwed it up, the part about us. I'm sorry, Alex. I'm so very sorry.

Do you remember when we met each other? You said that I always run away. You were right, Alex. I ran away, especially from myself and my feelings. And from you. But I don't want to run away anymore like a miserable coward!

I don't want to have a stone for a heart.

The rest I'd like to tell you in person, and I hope . . .

I hope.

I love you,

Mia

Chapter 23

Alexander

llllllllllllllllllllllllllllllllllllllllllllllllllllllllllllllllllllllllllllllllllllllllllllllllllllllllllllllllllll

"You got mail," my father said, pointing to a letter lying on the kitchen table. It was from Mia! What could she have to tell me that was important enough for her to write me a letter? I had a burning desire to tear the envelope open right then and there—but not with my dad sitting there.

I could feel his eyes on me, watching me without letting on. As if I might suddenly turn into a lifeless block of ice if he didn't watch out.

"How are you doing, son?" he asked.

Good grief, I was okay! I was still alive, wasn't I? "Already feeling fine again, thanks," I mumbled and bit into an apple. Lots of vitamins—that was supposed to help me recover as fast as possible. I was so sick of Grandma hovering around me constantly like a mother hen! When she found out I had gotten out of bed against her orders, she would make my life miserable. But I just couldn't stand being in bed anymore.

Lying around doing nothing wasn't good for me. In the quiet of my room, my thoughts rioted . . . those thoughts that had made me wake with a start, bathed in sweat, every night since the big scare.

The more I tried to ignore them, the deeper they ate their way into my brain, like a tumor, until they filled every nook and cranny of my head. Until just the one question burned in me . . .

Should I really ask my dad? I was afraid of the answer. A moment longer I hesitated, then it burst out of me: "When . . . when I was in the hole in the ice, I heard something. It seemed like someone was calling me. A woman."

Dad didn't say anything. My heart pounded like crazy, but there was no going back now. I just *had* to know!

"Mom isn't a photographer traveling around to different foreign countries, is she?" I asked quietly, and couldn't keep my voice from trembling. "She's dead. That's what happened."

My father didn't speak for a long while. He didn't look at me when he finally started to talk. "Yes. Katarina drowned in the river eleven years ago."

The sun still cast rings on the floor. Our kitchen looked just the way it had before. How was that possible, now that everything had changed in an instant? Now that I was finally sure. To hear Dad say aloud what I had hardly dared to think was a shock. It was as if his words, the sadness in his eyes, made it an irreversible reality: my mother was dead.

Now I could feel it with my fingertips like the grain of the wood of the kitchen table. I could smell it like the mellow, sweetness of Grandma's winter apples. Suddenly, I perceived everything around me with exceptional clarity. But at the same time, nothing seemed to fit together anymore. The apples. The rings of sunlight. Death.

"I . . . I don't understand. What happened to Mom?" I asked, confused.

"Yeah, what did happen?" my father sighed. He continued to sit and brood. I was just about to repeat my question when he finally started talking again: "The night that it happened, I woke up. The bed was empty next to me. Katarina was missing, and you kids, too."

Dad balled his hands into fists and opened them again, as if he were trying in vain to hold on to something precious that was running through his fingers like water. "The sight of your empty beds still haunts my dreams. I called, but no one answered. I searched the entire house but I couldn't find you. And then I found the letter. Katarina had written me that she couldn't stand it anymore. That she was going away and wanted to be free forever. And that she would take you with her. Finally, I ran like a crazy person, ran down to the edge of the river. It was a bright late summer night. An enormous full moon hung over the river, so low it seemed like you could touch it. Its cold light shone on the dark water and in your wide-open eyes. So I had found my little boys again, cowering together in the reeds. You were drenched to the bone, you and your brother. I tried to find out what had happened. You didn't make a sound the entire time, but Jay answered my questions. 'Mama went swimming,' he said. 'She wanted us to go in the water with her. But Skip said the water is too cold, and we don't want to . . .'"

I shuddered. I bit my teeth together to keep them from chattering. My father didn't notice; he continued the story.

"I brought you two into the house. Then I called Iris—someone had to stay with you. As soon as she arrived, I ran back outside to look for Katarina. I rowed the boat out on the river. I called for her, hoping desperately for an answer, even though reason told me that she was dead.

"Finally I found her. Drowned. She had gotten caught in the tangled roots of a weeping willow. I brought her to your island and rocked her in my arms until dawn. I was out of my mind with grief, but at some point, I grasped that she wouldn't come to life again. I . . . I didn't know what I should do. And I was afraid. Afraid of what people would say. That they would blame me for Katarina's death. Everyone in town knew we had problems and that we had fought more bitterly than ever that day. That I had hit Katarina. . . . The thought that someone might take you two away from me nearly made me lose my mind.

"I got Iris and we sat next to Katarina and grieved and thought about what we should do. She was scared, too, and she felt partially responsible for her daughter's death. So we buried Katarina on the island. In town, I told everyone that she had left us."

"But why all the lies? Why did you tell us for years and years that she was still alive?" I was about to hit him.

Dad couldn't look me in the eyes. "It was easier with Jay. He never asked about Katarina again. But you . . . you seemed to have completely forgotten that night at the river. Again and again, you drilled us: where did Mama go, and when was she coming back? How do you tell two little boys that their mother is never coming back? That she's dead? I just couldn't do it. And in the end, that's why I told you the tales about her travels."

My father looked at his hands lying in front of him on the table: big and powerless, like fish lying out to dry. There was dirt under his fingernails.

"Your grandmother warned me from the very beginning. 'There are no merciful lies, Eric,' she always preached. 'Only lies.' But I didn't listen to her. Maybe because I wanted so badly to believe them myself. I wanted to believe Katarina was strolling along a beach in a foreign country and not lying dead and buried in the ground."

"But that doesn't make any sense!" I contradicted hotly. "If Mom is really dead, then who sent me all those photographs?"

"Katarina had a close friend named Ruth, who had worked with her in the photography studio. They had always dreamed of traveling to exotic places together. Ruth did become a photojournalist. Although she was on the road a lot, the two of them stayed in touch until Katarina died. Ruth was very upset about her death. Apart from your grandmother, she was the only one I told the truth. 'You can come to me any time you need help, Eric,' she offered. And when you constantly demanded to know why your mother didn't write to you . . ."

"You asked Ruth to do it."

"Exactly. Ruth was happy to do it. It probably made her feel like she could do something for Katarina. And I thought, what could be the harm? You were so happy every time you got mail." He shook his head. "I didn't want to ruin that for you. You were just a kid! I thought you could handle the truth better when you were a little older. 'Next year I'll talk to them,' I swore again and again. But instead of getting easier, it got even harder over time. And every time I found a new excuse to avoid speaking up.

"Until this year, your grandmother insisted that this game finally had to end. 'Alexander is almost an adult now!' she said. I knew she was right. So I called Ruth and asked her not to send anymore pictures. But I didn't manage to talk with you boys. After all these years . . . I just didn't know where to start. I guess the whole thing snowballed out of control," he confessed. "I'm sorry, Alexander."

"I think some part of me has always sensed that she's dead," I said slowly. "The traveling, the photos—that was a beautiful dream that I held on to. But I guess you have to wake up sometime, right?"

"Yes. At some point you have to wake up, even if it hurts."

I swallowed, and forced out the words that were eating me up inside, burning a hole in my soul: "Do you think . . . do you think Katarina . . . Mom . . . wanted to kill us?" My voice sounded unfamiliar in my own ears, frail and thin like a child's.

"I've asked myself that question so many times," Dad finally responded. "Even after all these years, I don't have an answer to it. I can't tell you. I wasn't there."

Despite the sunshine streaming through the kitchen windows, I was cold. I was freezing—still stuck in that hole in the ice. "The only thing I can remember is this image of her standing knee-deep in the water of the river and waving at us to come to her," I whispered haltingly. "Then nothing else."

For a short moment, my father placed his hand on mine and squeezed it. "Maybe it's better if some things are left in the dark and forgotten," he said gently. "Your grandmother always thought it was a blessing God granted you two."

We sat in the kitchen together for a while longer, not saying anything, and listened to the plastic fish sing for us. And it didn't matter at all that we were crying.

Chapter 24

Jay

|||||||||||||||||||||||||||||||||||||||||||||||||||||||||||||||||||||||||||||||||||||||||||||||||||||||||||||||||||||||||

One day recently, Mia appeared at our front door with her cello. My brother led her up to his room, and they stayed there for a long time. Mia made the cello sing for him. Her singing heart.

No, I didn't eavesdrop on them on purpose! But the deep tones resonated in the brittle bones of our house. I stood downstairs in the foyer and could feel them when I put my hand on the banister.

That's how everything had begun: with this sound that drew me to Mia's window, into a new and different life. The music was like melting snow on my face. And although I knew it wasn't meant for me, I had to smile.

~~~~~

I would have liked to thank Mia for everything she had given me. I got my chance a few days later when we bumped into each other in our kitchen. "I have a present for you," I said. Mia studied the CD I slipped into her hand with curiosity.

"Jay's Four Seasons," she read. "These are your recordings?" I nodded. Everything was on the CD, our entire last year in a nutshell: my springtime birds; the singing fish above our kitchen table; Grandma's vigorous clanging of pots and pans; the murmur of the river; the heavy summer silence, interrupted by ripe cherries falling from the tree; the jingling of Mia's shell earrings; the splashing of the dives at Skip's birthday party; then the screeching of a kingfisher; the crackling of frost.

And for the finale, the sound of a cello, like the distant hope that it will soon be spring again.

"Thank you, Jay," Mia said, and seemed to be unsure whether or not she should hug me. "You know, Alex and I are thinking about maybe going to the ocean for a few days during spring break," she related, trying in vain not to let the anticipation be heard in her voice. "Well, I don't know yet if it will work out. But if it does, we'll bring you a recording of the pounding surf. That's a promise!"

"That would be great." I smiled at her.

"Gosh, Jay, you seem so . . . different." Mia studied me with amazement, like a familiar map where the roads had suddenly changed course. "It's your left eye, the brown one!" she finally decided. "Usually when we were talking to each other, I always had the feeling it was looking right through me." She laughed, as if her words seemed a little silly even to herself. "As if only half of you was here, and the other half was somewhere far, far away. As if your brown eye were actually looking at someone completely different."

She was right. "It was always watching Alina," I admitted. "But not anymore."

She was quiet for a while, searching for the words. "The old legends are filled with river spirits and mermaids and . . ."

"No one believes in that kind of stuff!" I interrupted her.

"That might be exactly the point: no one believes in them anymore!" Mia exclaimed. Her hands drew exclamation points behind her sentences. "But maybe it was the people believing in all these creatures that made them real and powerful in the first place. What if it's the same with Alina? Who knows, maybe you brought her to life, Jay!"

"Me?" I asked, feeling as if I had just stepped into a mudhole and felt the ground slipping away under my feet.

"Yes, you! I mean, Katarina died when you were still very young. That must have been hard for you. You must have wished she was still with you."

Oh, how I had wished that! And then at some point, Alina was just there. There for me like a star that blossomed in the night. Had my wishes alone given her form? Had my thousand vows of loyalty been the blood that first made her heart beat?

Promise you'll never forget me, Jay!

I can't exist without you, Jay!

And then I realized that Mia's suggestion wasn't so absurd, after all.

"So you mean I conjured the spirit of my mother." I looked out the kitchen window, toward the river, shining in the weak light of the winter sun like a tentative greeting. The willows along the shore cowered, freezing in the sharp wind. "I only know that Alina is still out there," I said quietly. "Weaker now, only a shadow of what she was. She's unhappy and lonely. That's the only reason she tried to take Skip into the river with her. What on earth should I do now, Mia?"

Her smile was warm and encouraging like the sound of a cello. "Only you can decide that, Jay. But I think you already know what you have to do, don't you?"

≈≈≈≈≈

Yes, I knew. That evening, I stood on the dock when the blue twilight came. With it came Alina. Her pale reflection wavered on the water like the sputtering flame of a candle.

She was silent. There was nothing to hear but the rustling of the wind and the constant dripping of water from the willow twigs. They were already starting to bud.

I found it hard to speak into the expectant silence. "I want to talk with you, Alina!" I said loudly. "Until recently I thought you were the one holding on to me. But I see now that's not true. I didn't want to let go of you, either."

The trees along the shore creaked their disapproval of my idiocy. I could feel tears forming in my eyes. "That was wrong, Alina. No one can keep things from changing. The river can't stop moving. And people, too . . . they learn, they love, they grow up. Or they die, that happens, too. People can't stay the way they are forever. No one can! It's not natural, and it's dangerous. And that's why . . . that's why it's time for me to say good-bye to you," I managed to croak in spite of the lump in my throat, and the knots in my heart.

"I release you, Alina. I'm letting you be Katarina again and go to the ocean." Slowly, I raised my hand to wave to Alina, and she waved, too . . . waved back one last time.

A gust of wind blew through the branches like a sigh. It gave the river's surface goose bumps and made the image of Alina quiver. Its outline blurred in the dark water and dissolved.

And then she was gone, forever.

There was nothing on the water but my own reflection.

Acknowledgments

A big, fat thank you goes to my godmother Dida, who always believed in me. Through her constructive critique, she helped me set this story on the right path.

To Sophia and Nadja for seriously engaging with my strange questions ("What do you associate with blood oaths?")

To my family, many thanks for your understanding and your great support.

Furthermore, I'd like to thank my friends and critics Julia, Johannes v.D and others for pointing out that dimples aren't located at the corners of the mouth, and Anissa for her lists of mistakes. As well as Johnny, who eagerly beats the advertising drum for me, and my most loyal "fans," the Jorkowski family. Thanks also to Zoran Drvenkar, who as a professional found time to read through the first chapters.

Above all, I thank my editor, Ulrike Metzger, who with clear vision and enthusiasm helped make this novel a success.

About the Author

Author Marlene Röder was awarded the Hans-im-Glück prize by the city of Limburg, Germany, for her debut novel, *Im Fluss*, the German edition of **In the River Darkness**. For her second critically acclaimed novel, **Zebraland**, she received two more awards, including the Hans-Jörg-Martin Award for Best Youth Crime Novel. She has also published a short story collection and currently lives in Limburg, Germany.

© Fotopoetin Jen Preusler